The Case of Capital Intrigue

Nancy suddenly found herself alone with the golden hummingbird. She went back over to the table to admire it. Picking it up gently, she found it was incredibly heavy for such a delicate object. As she set the bird back down, Nancy thought she heard someone approaching. She went to the door, but no one seemed to be around.

Nancy walked back into the Reception Room. I suppose I could at least be helpful, she thought. She took George's light meter and held it in front of the hummingbird. The lighting was fine, maybe too bright.

Suddenly, Nancy noticed the light meter's needle fall. A shadow had been cast over the hummingbird, and it was coming from behind her.

Nancy began to turn around. "Who's there?" she said.

That's when she felt something slam into the back of her head. She tried to keep her balance but fell to the ground, helpless and unconscious.

Nancy Drew
Mystery Stories

Available from MINSTREL Books

NANCY DREW® 142

THE CASE OF CAPITAL INTRIGUE

CAROLYN KEENE

A MINSTREL® BOOK

Published by POCKET BOOKS
New York   London   Toronto   Sydney   Tokyo   Singapore

This book is a work of fiction. Names, characters, places and incidents are products of the author's imagination or are used fictitiously. Any resemblance to actual events or locales or persons living or dead is entirely coincidental.

A MINSTREL PAPERBACK *Original*

A Minstrel Book published by
POCKET BOOKS, a division of Simon & Schuster Inc.
1230 Avenue of the Americas, New York, NY 10020

Copyright © 1998 by Simon & Schuster Inc.
Produced by Mega-Books, Inc.

ISBN: 0-671-00751-3

First Minstrel Books printing April 1998

10 9 8 7 6 5 4 3 2 1

Cover art by Ernie Norcia

Printed in the U.S.A.

Contents

1

Shocking News

"Taxi! Taxi!" Nancy Drew waved down a cab and, when the yellow car stopped in front of her, climbed inside. She tossed her long, reddish-blond hair over her shoulder and settled back gratefully in her seat.

"Where to?" the driver asked, glancing at her in his rearview mirror.

"The White House, please. The visitor's entrance," Nancy replied, trying to sound as if she took a taxi to the White House every day of the week.

The city of Washington, D.C., spread out before her as the taxi hummed over the Fourteenth Street Bridge. To Nancy's right, a sleek racing shell cut down the Potomac River, its eight oarsmen rowing in perfect unison.

Washington was nothing like Chicago, Nancy mused. Chicago was the nearest big city to her hometown of River Heights. In Chicago sleek concrete-and-glass skyscrapers edged the skyline. But in D.C., only the graceful, white granite obelisk of the Washington Monument seemed to touch the sky.

When Nancy's friend George Fayne had snagged an internship as a photographer's assistant at the White House, she had immediately invited Nancy to visit. Nancy hadn't needed to be asked twice. Finally reaching her destination, Nancy's mind began to imagine the days and nights ahead: witnessing the political process from behind the scenes, attending parties, meeting other interns . . .

Suddenly, Nancy was thrown back into the present as the taxi driver gunned the engine to make it through a yellow light at an intersection. The cab crossed the center of the Mall, home of some of the country's most famous monuments—including Washington's, Jefferson's, Lincoln's, and the Vietnam War Memorial. As she looked at the horizon, the dome of the U.S. Capitol rose through the late-morning haze.

To her left, Nancy caught a glimpse of the White House before it disappeared behind an enormous, dark sandstone building. That glance started her heart pounding with excitement.

I am going to the White House, and I am *not* going as a tourist, she reminded herself proudly. Instinctively, she smoothed her hair and brushed a few flecks of imaginary fuzz from her blazer.

The cab stopped at the corner of Seventeenth Street and Pennsylvania Avenue. "Say hello to the president for me," the taxi driver said as he lifted her suitcase out of the trunk.

"Will do," Nancy replied. She felt so good, she tipped him an extra dollar.

She wove her way through the noisy crowd of tourists, trying to stay out of the pictures they were taking of one another in front of America's first home. Finally she arrived at the nine-foot-high wrought-iron visitor's gate.

A handsome marine in full Honor Guard dress blues stepped from the guardhouse behind the gate. "May I help you, Miss?"

"Hi. I'm Nancy Drew. I'm here to see George Fayne in the White House Photo Office."

The marine ran a white-gloved finger over a clipboard list, his finger stopping about halfway down. He looked up and said, "I'll need to see your driver's license and social security card,

3

please, Ms. Drew." The guard opened one half of the gate and gestured for Nancy to come through. "I'll also need to check the contents of your suitcase."

After a few minutes, the guard returned Nancy's luggage and handed her a laminated blue pass marked with a big *A*. "Please display this pass at all times while in the White House," he said. "You may proceed to the West Wing straight ahead. Enjoy your visit."

Nancy thanked him and made her way down the long, covered driveway framed by slender white columns. The door was guarded by another marine. He saluted her, ceremoniously clicked his heels together, and pivoted to open the door with practiced military efficiency. I feel like royalty, Nancy thought.

Inside, everything was silent and still. The West Wing lobby had the air of an old luxury hotel, complete with marble columns, polished antique furniture, and thick carpeting. Nancy paused and took a deep breath. "Well, here I am," she murmured to herself, feeling just a little daunted by the fact.

An elderly woman emerged as if from nowhere. "Of course you are, dear," she said kindly. "But the question is, Who are you?"

Nancy laughed, relieved by the woman's sense

of humor. "Nancy Drew," she said. "I'm here to see George Fayne in the photographer's office."

"Certainly. Please have a seat, and I'll let him know you're here."

"Her," Nancy corrected the woman.

"Her?"

"Yes, ma'am," Nancy said very politely. "My friend George is a girl."

The elderly woman's face lit up. "Oh, *that* George," she said.

Nancy sat down in a deeply cushioned wing chair and chuckled to think that George had already made herself known. It wasn't long before her friend came striding through a set of double doors at the far end of the lobby. Her collar-length dark curls bounced with each long step of her gait. George stopped a few feet in front of Nancy and placed her hands on her hips.

"So, it's true," George said, a wry smile on her face. "They'll let just anyone in here!"

The two friends laughed and embraced in a hug.

"Seriously," George said. "I'm so glad you're here." She lowered her voice to a whisper. "It'll be a relief to be able to talk to someone I know I can trust."

"What do you mean?" Nancy asked, her curiosity immediately aroused.

George led the way out of the lobby. "You thought *I* was competitive," she continued. "You should see the people who work here. There's nothing they wouldn't do to get what they want." George pointed to a cloakroom off the hall. "You can put your suitcase in there for now."

"You've gotten awfully cynical in just one week, George," Nancy said as they were on their way again.

"Not at all," George protested. "I've just found my niche!"

The girls broke out laughing again as they approached a set of mahogany double doors. The doors opened onto a wide hallway with maroon carpeting and beige walls. At the far end, two men in dark suits were having a quiet discussion that could not be heard over the sounds of clicking keyboards coming from the offices.

"Not very glamorous," George admitted. "This is the first floor of the West Wing, and it's all business. The president's highest ranking staff members have their offices here and on the second floor. I'll give you the official tour of the residence later."

"The residence?"

"That's what we call the White House itself. The West Wing was added on decades ago just to provide working space. But the rooms in the

6

White House"—George placed her hand on her chest, as if calming her heart—"are unbelievably gorgeous."

"And the president lives—"

"Second and third floor of the White House," George answered. "I'm afraid we won't be touring those rooms."

"So which one of these high-ranking offices is yours?" Nancy asked, teasing.

"Big shot that I am, I get a basement cubicle," George quipped. "Listen to this: my official title is First Assistant to the Chief Photographer of the White House Archives."

"Impressive," Nancy said sincerely.

"My boss, Joe Newman, is one of the nicest people I've met here," George said. "We've got a big photo shoot at three this afternoon. You'll get to see him—and me—in action." She stopped outside an open door. A red velvet rope hung over the threshold. "Take a peek, Nan. It's the Oval Office."

Nancy peered into the huge room. The president was not at his desk, but the room was still awe-inspiring. Nancy noted that a rug the size of a swimming pool covered the floor. The presidential seal was woven into the middle of it. "Wow!" was all that Nancy could manage.

"Come on. Now I'll show you my office."

George led Nancy down another hall and a flight of stairs. "Then we'll call for some lunch. Thursday is enchilada day."

George's office turned out be one in a row of at least a dozen cubicles barely bigger than walk-in closets. On the corridor wall outside her office hung scores of one-by-two-foot photographs of the president and his staff.

"Those are called *jumbos*," George said. "We catch the president and his staff going through all their daily activities. New pics get posted here every week. The old ones go to staff offices upstairs. Taking them down and putting up new ones is part of my job."

George turned toward her cubicle. "Have a look while I call in our lunch."

Nancy studied the photographs. They looked like what she might see in the newspaper or on the news. One showed the president, seated at a massive desk with somber-looking men and women standing in a semicircle behind him. To the president's left, a tall, elegantly dressed woman held open a wooden case, as if offering the president a cigar. Nancy looked more closely and saw they weren't cigars. They were fountain pens. Nancy remembered hearing that after the president signed important documents, he gave away the pens he'd used as souvenirs of the event.

A burst of noise caused Nancy to look up and see two men about her age emerge from an office down the hall. They were impeccably dressed, and one of them carried a fairly large cardboard box.

As they caught up to Nancy, the one with the box stopped. He smiled at her and nodded toward the wall of photographs. "So, what's the commander in chief up to today?" he asked.

Nancy pretended to scrutinize the picture. "Looks to me like he's busy ensuring world peace and democracy," she said.

The young man laughed, a lock of his straw-colored hair falling over his eyes. "That's good to hear." He shifted the box under one arm and extended his hand. "I'm Brent Larson, and this is my friend Eduardo Enriquez."

"I'm Nancy Drew, here visiting my friend George Fayne. Do you know her?"

"Sure we do," Brent said.

Nancy guessed that Brent was a little over six feet tall. He wore a charcoal gray suit, a crisp, white cotton shirt, and a tightly knotted tie patterned with tiny aquamarine fish, whose color perfectly matched his eyes.

Just as Nancy was about to ask him another question, George popped out of her cubicle.

"Nice tie, Larson," George said. "You trying to swim with the sharks, or what?"

"Anything to impress you, George," Brent replied.

"Oh, yeah?" George said. "Well, keep trying. I'll let you know when it works."

Nancy saw Brent begin to blush and decided to come to his rescue. "So," she said, "you and Eduardo both work here in the White House?"

"Please, call me Eddie." Brent's friend had jet black hair and emerald green eyes.

"I work down the hall in the Administration Office," Brent said. "I'm in charge of commissioning presidential gifts and art."

"That sounds like a great job," Nancy said. "Do you have a title as impressive as George's to go with it?"

"Oh, most certainly," Brent said. "I am the Deputy Director of Executive Gifts, Acquisitions, and Honoraria. You may call me His Royal Deputy Giftness."

Laughing, Nancy asked, "How did you ever get such a job?"

"My father owns a New York auction house," Brent said, somewhat sheepishly. "I guess you could say it's in my blood."

George jumped in. "And Eddie here is studying at Georgetown University, right?"

"Yes." Eddie smiled, and suddenly his whole face changed from its previous serious intensity to welcoming good humor. "I'm from San Valente, a small country in South America. I'm studying political science while my family lives here in Washington."

"What Eddie's not telling you," Brent interrupted, "is that his father is an ambassador from San Valente. His parents will be staying in the Lincoln Bedroom after the state dinner this week—as the president's personal guests."

"Oh, on the second floor of the residence," Nancy said knowingly.

"I see George has taught you the White House lingo already," Brent said. "Eddie's my pass to get up there with this." He held the cardboard box out, obviously waiting to be asked what was inside.

"Okay," George said, scowling in mock exasperation. "What's in the box?"

Brent carefully cradled the box on one arm and opened the top with his other hand. "Check it out," he said, lowering it before George and Nancy.

Inside was a church scene in plaster of two families in adjoining pews. The women and children sat primly, while the two men stood shaking hands over the back of the bench.

"It's called *Neighboring Pews*," Brent said. "De-

11

signed around 1860 by John Rogers. The Secret Service called me a few days ago and said the maid had accidentally broken the one in the Lincoln Suite."

"Oops," George said. "But this doesn't look broken," she noted.

Brent shook his head as he closed the box. "Rogers made thousands of them. I rounded this one up with only a few phone calls, and when I said it was for the First Family's living quarters, the owner let me have it for free."

"Nice going, Brent," Nancy said.

At that moment the phone in George's office rang. She ducked into her cubicle to get it.

Nancy was about to ask Eddie about his father's relationship to the president when they heard George cry out, "What? Oh, no!"

They crowded into the doorway of George's cubicle. She sat with her back to them, still on the phone.

"Okay," she said into the receiver, and hung up.

George slowly turned around in her chair. Her face was pale. "It's about Joe Newman, my boss," she said in a shaky voice. "He's in the hospital in critical condition."

2

A Precious Gift

"What happened?" Brent asked George. "Is Joe going to be okay?"

George took a deep breath to calm herself. "He was mugged outside his apartment in Georgetown."

"Mugged?" Nancy asked. "A mugger put him in intensive care? Did they catch the culprit?"

"Are you sure it was just a mugging?" Eddie said. "It sounds as if someone wanted to harm Joe."

"Yes, it was just a mugger, and no, no one caught him—or her, I suppose," George said.

"Do you need to go to the hospital, George?"

Nancy asked, reaching around her friend's shoulder to give her some support.

"No," George replied. "They only let close family members into the intensive care unit. The word from the front office is 'Carry on.'"

Brent set the box holding the plaster tableau on George's desk and took her hand in his. "Listen," he said. "I'm sure Joe's going to be all right. He's where he can get the help he needs. But you know what this means, don't you?"

Everyone turned to Brent.

"It means," he continued, "that you're going to have to do the shoot alone this afternoon."

"I'll call someone to take over, if you don't think I can handle it," George said, somewhat defensively.

Brent cringed. "I'm sorry, George. It's just that everything has to go right this afternoon. It's important. Remember, it's at three o'clock in the Reception Room."

Eddie checked his watch and cleared his throat. "You must forgive my friend, George," he said smoothly. "He is obsessed with the shoot and everything else. You will do a fine job. And now we have to attend to the Lincoln Bedroom."

"Don't worry," Nancy said. "You go replace that statue. We'll be ready by three."

"Okay, good." Brent smiled at George, trying to cheer her up. "We'll see you then."

Eddie said goodbye politely, and the two young men disappeared out into the hall.

George sank back into her chair. "I can't believe it. Three weeks ago photography was just a hobby for me. Now I'm in charge of shooting an important diplomatic event. And poor Joe . . ."

Before Nancy could say anything encouraging, George slammed her palms down hard on the desk top. "I can do this," she said, standing up. "I'll show Brent Larson. And when we do visit Joe in the hospital, I'll be able to tell him everything went off without a hitch."

Ten minutes later the girls had picked up their lunch from the West Wing dining hall and were back in George's office.

"I'm really not that hungry after all," George said, pushing her plate away. "I guess I'm too upset about Joe. And too nervous about the shoot."

"George, you're great with a camera," Nancy said. "You'll do fine, but will you please tell me what is so important about this shoot? Everyone seems so tense about it."

"Oh, Nan!" George exclaimed. "I forgot, you don't know. I'm sorry."

Nancy nodded.

15

"Here's the scoop," George began. "The United States and Eddie's country, San Valente, have finally worked out an economic agreement. Apparently, they've been negotiating this deal for nearly a year."

"No wonder Eddie's father and the president have gotten so close."

"Right," George replied. "Anyway, the president of San Valente sent our president some amazing thank-you gift, and we're supposed to photograph it today along with some of the negotiators from both countries. Just posed stuff, nothing candid."

"So, just what is this amazing gift?" Nancy asked.

"I don't know," George replied.

"You don't know?"

George rolled her eyes. "Brent has gone totally nuts over it. He's in charge of taking care of whatever it is until it officially changes hands at a state dinner the day after tomorrow. But Brent won't let on what the gift is."

"Is it top secret?" Nancy asked, her eyes twinkling.

"Don't get too excited," George warned. "It's top secret only in Brent's mind, and only until three o'clock." George checked her watch. There was still plenty of time to plan the shoot. Suddenly a thought occurred to her. "How does he expect me to know what equipment to bring if I don't even know what I'm shooting?" she said, her voice rising.

At that moment a young woman poked her head into the cubicle. "Sorry to bother you, George," she said. "I've got a message from Darcy. She says the shoot has been moved up to one-thirty. Better get going."

The woman left and Nancy jumped up, brushing crumbs from her short blue skirt. "I'm ready. Just tell me what to do."

George, however, hadn't moved. "That Darcy," she mumbled, putting on her official White House blue blazer. "She did this on purpose."

"What are you talking about?" Nancy asked.

"Come on. I'll fill you in on the way," George said.

After two hallways, one gray steel fire door, and one Secret Service checkpoint, Nancy broke into George's tense silence. "Is this when you start filling me in?" she asked.

"Oh," George said in frustration. "I'm sorry *again*, Nan. I'm just so mad, I can't think straight."

"Well, let me help," Nancy volunteered. "For starters, where are we going?"

At that, George cracked a smile. "I sure am glad you came to visit, Nancy." Pointing, she continued, "This tunnel leads underground to the Old Executive Office Building, that big ugly building across the street from the White House. That's where the fabulous, wonderful, VIP Darcy O'Neill's office is."

Nancy laughed at her friend's sarcasm. "And just why is this Darcy so fabulous?" she inquired.

"For some reason, she's decided she wants my job," George explained. "She works in the White House Advance Office now, scheduling presidential phone calls and itineraries—important stuff—but she wants me out and herself in as Joe's assistant."

Nancy put her hand on George's arm to slow down her gait. "You don't think you're being just a little paranoid?" she asked.

"Wait and see," George answered.

Minutes later they emerged from the tunnel into another office building. A few potted plants and some old, dark oil paintings covered with spidery cracks were the only decoration.

George stopped abruptly beside an office door with a surveillance camera mounted outside. She glared into the camera's lens as she sharply rapped on the door.

A syrupy-sweet soprano voice responded, "Do come in, Ms. Fayne." A buzzer signaled that the door was unlocked.

18

George whispered to Nancy, "That voice is like nails on blackboard to me," and proceeded inside.

A tiny young woman sat at a large, extremely neat desk. She was dressed as tidily as the desk, and every strand of her burnished red hair was exactly in place. On the desk stood a nameplate that read "Ms. Darcy O'Neill." A smiley-face sticker sat in the middle of the *O*. She certainly didn't look like the ogre George had described.

Darcy held out two laminated cards. "Here, I have your special passes for the Reception Room all ready."

Instead of taking the passes, George crossed her arms in front of her chest. "I don't suppose you had anything to do with the shoot being moved up?"

"Whatever do you mean?" Darcy asked innocently.

"I mean that I've got less than fifteen minutes to get over to the Reception Room with all my equipment."

Darcy's eyes lit up with mock surprise. "Silly," she said. "The shoot's not until three o'clock."

George's jaw dropped. "I just got a message from you saying that it had been moved up to one-thirty."

"There must have been some kind of miscommunication," she said sweetly. "I didn't send such a message." She extended the passes to Nancy. "You must be Nancy Drew, from River Heights."

Nancy took the passes. "Yes, I am."

"You know, George," Darcy said, smoothing her already perfect hair, "I have a considerable amount of photographic experience. Perhaps I should take the time from my own busy job to help you this afternoon."

"Thanks, Darcy," George said, her jaw clenched. "But I think we can handle it."

"Well, just let me know. I'll be here."

George was steaming on the way back to the West Wing. "Can you believe that?"

"She seemed pretty nice to me," Nancy said.

George stared at her friend in disbelief.

"Just kidding, George," Nancy quickly added.

"She has what's called West Wing Envy," George said. "She'll do anything to get out of the Old Executive Office Building and over here, including giving me a heart attack by telling me the wrong time for an important shoot."

"Well, at least now we have plenty of time to get ready," Nancy observed.

Which turned out to be what they needed. It took them two trips to lug all the lights, screens, and cameras over to the White House, but by two-thirty they had everything ready to go.

The Diplomatic Reception Room was an impressive sight, furnished in gold and white. The walls were adorned with large murals of the American landscape framed in gold. The ceiling practically dripped with glittering gold-and-bronze antique chandeliers, and the floor was covered with a rug bearing symbols of each of the fifty states.

Brent and Eddie appeared at two-forty, escorted by a stern-looking Secret Service agent. Brent introduced the agent as Don Marks, head of Residence Security. He stood in the middle of the room, his hands shoved deep into his pockets, watching as Brent set a square wooden crate on a side table.

"If you're all set here," Marks suddenly said, "I'm going over to the West Wing to make sure there's space in the safe for that thing."

"Yeah, thanks," Brent said, with a wave of his hand. He took a penknife out of his pocket and pried off the lid of the crate. From the middle of a nest of packing material, he gently lifted out the gift from the president of San Valente.

"Oh, it's gorgeous," Nancy gasped. She understood why Don Marks had escorted Brent to the room. The gift was a solid gold hummingbird about ten inches tall.

Brent turned the bird this way and that for everyone to see.

"It looks old," George said. She turned to

Eddie. "Does the hummingbird mean something special in your country?"

"It's considered very good luck to see one," Eddie replied. "They're supposed to bring peace and prosperity."

Brent placed the bird on a side table. The figure had delicate, twiglike legs and a long beak. The surface of the bird was perfectly smooth, with no feathers etched into the precious metal, and its wings were raised as if preparing for flight.

"This sculpture is at least seven or eight hundred years old," Brent said. "When the Spanish conquered San Valente some five hundred years ago, they melted down all the gold they could find and shipped it back to Spain. This piece survived and is very rare."

Eddie stepped forward. "There are some people in my country who believe this bird should not be given away. It is a national treasure."

"And how do you feel about that?" Nancy asked.

Eddie shrugged his shoulders. "It's not important how I feel."

Brent interrupted. "The President of the United States can't personally accept gifts like this anyway. The bird is just going from a museum in San Valente to a museum here in the White House."

"That's one way to look at it. Excuse me,

please," Eddie said abruptly, and strode out of the room.

"Hold on, Eddie." Brent started after his friend. "He's got to be here for the pictures," he called to George. "Finish setting up, and I'll be right back." Then he disappeared out the door.

George knelt down and dug around in her camera bag. "Oh, no," she moaned, pulling equipment out frantically.

"What is it?"

"If Brent had at least told me that the gift was so small, I'd have brought my telephoto lens," George said angrily. "It's back in my cube, and the bigwigs will be here any minute."

"Let me get it for you," Nancy offered.

"No," George insisted. "You'd never find it in that disaster area. I know right where it is. Be right back."

Nancy suddenly found herself alone with the golden hummingbird. She went back over to the table to admire it. Picking it up gently, she found it was incredibly heavy for such a delicate object. As she set the bird back down, Nancy thought she heard someone approaching. She went to the door, expecting to see Eddie or Brent, but no one seemed to be around.

Nancy walked back into the Reception Room. I suppose I could at least be helpful, she thought.

She took George's light meter and held it in front of the hummingbird. The lighting was fine, maybe too bright. Suddenly, Nancy noticed the light meter's needle fall. A shadow had been cast over the hummingbird, and it was coming from behind her.

Nancy began to turn around. "Who's there?" she said. That's when she felt something slam into the back of her head, sending a searing blade of pain down her spine. She tried to keep her balance but fell to the ground, helpless and unconscious.

3

A Thief in the White House

The first thing Nancy saw when she came to was an enormous chandelier looming high above her. The tiny points of light fuzzed in and out of focus, and then there was George, kneeling over her.

"Nan? Nancy? Are you okay?"

Nancy sat up. Her head throbbed in pain with each heartbeat. "Something . . . somebody hit me in the back of the head—hard."

"Can you stand?"

"Yes, I think so," Nancy replied calmly.

George helped her friend to her feet.

Nancy swept her hair out of her eyes and rubbed the back of her neck. "Someone came up behind me. I didn't even have time to react."

"We've got to get you to a doctor."

Nancy tried to smile. "No, no. I'm okay—no dizziness or anything."

At that moment Brent came back into the room. "I can't find Eddie anywhere. Hey, what's up?" He rushed over to where the girls were standing, next to the side table. "Where's the bird?"

Nancy and George looked at the empty table in horror. "Oh, no," Nancy said. "It's gone!"

"If this is some kind of joke, it isn't funny." Brent glanced frantically around the room.

"Do you see us laughing?" George asked. "Somebody just attacked Nancy."

"And obviously stole the statue," Nancy added.

"No way. It's not possible," Brent cried. "I was only gone for a couple of minutes. Come on, George. Tell me this isn't happening."

George just glared at Brent.

"Hey, Larson. Where's this fantastic bird thing?" a voice boomed out, filling the Reception Room.

Nancy saw Brent's spine stiffen as a tall, lanky-framed man came in, his long-legged walk almost a lope. His charming smile disappeared when he saw Brent's expression.

"What's wrong, Larson? You look like somebody just died."

Brent didn't answer.

26

"Nancy, meet Todd Willis," George said. "He's on the National Security Council staff—you know, foreign policy, negotiations, intelligence, all the cloak-and-dagger stuff."

Todd strode forward and shook Nancy's hand, stating his title. "Deputy Chief Assistant to South American Bureau Chief Felicia Bingham. Pleased to meet you." He took a quick look around. "What's going on?"

Nancy explained that she'd just been knocked out and that the bird was stolen.

"We've got to notify Secret Service to seal off the residence before anyone gets out," George said.

"Wait," Brent said, staring into the empty wooden crate as if the bird might magically reappear at any moment. "If the press gets hold of this, it'll be a total embarrassment to the administration. There could be repercussions if it gets out."

But Todd was already on his cell phone. He explained the situation in sharp, clear sentences. Nancy was impressed by how calm he was. He covered the mouthpiece of the phone with his hand and whispered over to Brent, "Don't worry. I'm getting Marks involved. He'll know how to handle this.

"Yes, sir," Todd said into his phone. "Right away." He flipped the phone shut and put it back in his pocket. "The head of Residence Security, Don Marks, wants to see the two of you in his West Wing office now," he said, gesturing to Nancy and George. "Brent, listen up. Your job is to keep quiet about this. Marks has put special agents at the metal detectors at all the entrances. No one can get out of the White House with that statue."

Todd pulled out his cell phone again. "Now for damage control. I've got to call my boss and make up some story about why we aren't doing the shoot this afternoon."

Nancy and George began to pack up the photo equipment but were quickly interrupted.

"Hey, ladies," Todd said, "did you hear what I said? Marks's office—*now*. We'll get someone else to take all this stuff down."

Brent left the Diplomatic Reception Room with George and Nancy. The three of them could still hear Todd's booming voice inside. "Chief Bingham? It's Todd. I'm glad you haven't left to come over to the residence yet. Yes, yes. Well, there's a small problem with the photo session. . . ."

No one said anything until Nancy and George turned down the corridor to Don Marks's office.

"It's my fault. I shouldn't have left the room," Brent said. "That hummingbird was my responsibility."

28

"But who inside the White House would want to take it?" Nancy asked. "Who even knew where it would be this afternoon?"

Brent scratched his head. His blond hair now looked tousled, and the knot in his tie was askew. "Everyone in the Advance Office knew about my schedule," he said. "And so did most of the higher-ups involved in the negotiations with San Valente. A lot of people, actually."

"Don't panic," George said. "We'll get it back. My friend Nancy here has some experience with this sort of emergency."

Brent gave George a weak smile. "That's good," he said. "Because we've only got until the state dinner two nights from now. If we don't catch whoever did this and get the bird back by then, we can all kiss our jobs goodbye, and probably the agreement with San Valente as well."

A group of young staffers, talking and laughing loudly, came out of an office. Brent clammed up and backed against the wall, giving them room to pass.

When the hall was clear again, Brent continued, his voice low. "Are you going to the wild horse fund-raiser tonight, George?"

"I haven't had time to think about it, Brent. Doesn't it cost a lot to get in?"

"A hundred bucks a head. Come on, both of you. I'll pay for it." Brent took out a pen and a notepad. "It's at the Madison Hotel near Capitol Hill." He handed the slip of paper to George. "You can fill me in on what Don Marks has to say, and besides, it would be fun if you two were there."

George hastily stuffed the directions in her blazer pocket. "We'll see," she said. "It's been a long day, and Nancy's probably tired."

Nancy shook her head. "I'm fine." She grabbed George by the wrist and started to tow her down the hall. With a wave to Brent, Nancy called out "We'll see you tonight. And with any luck we'll have good news to share.

"Somebody has a crush on you," Nancy observed as she led George away.

"Oh, no, no," George said, shaking her head. "Brent's in love with Darcy O'Neill."

Before Nancy could reply, they arrived at Don Marks's office. George opened the door and walked right in.

Marks's secretary asked their names, then waved them on to an inner office, where the hulking Secret Service agent stood behind his desk, talking on the phone.

". . . I'm going through the background checks of all the staff right now. Yep, that's right. As soon as possible." Marks motioned for the girls to sit in the two hard-backed chairs in front of his desk.

As Nancy sat down, she noticed framed pictures of the previous three presidents on the back wall. They each showed the chief executive standing with Agent Marks, and each had the president's signature under it.

Marks hung up the phone and sat down at his desk. He adjusted his computer screen and started typing in information.

"George Fayne," he said, more to himself than to George. "Five foot eight, eighteen years old, from River Heights. You run track, play basketball and volleyball, and you've been working here just over three weeks. Correct?"

George nodded. "Yes, that's all true."

Marks glanced at Nancy. "Ms. Drew. Five foot seven, eighteen years old, also from River Heights. Hmmm." Marks paused for a moment, then scrolled down the screen. "You have a pilot's license?"

"Yes," Nancy answered. "I do." She was a little surprised that Marks knew so much about her, even though she imagined that extensive background checks were necessary for anyone working inside the White House.

"I also see a letter of reference here from a Chief McGinnis of the River Heights Police Department. He says you've helped his department solve a number of crimes. That's unusual, don't you think?"

"I suppose," Nancy said noncommitally. She noticed a cardboard box on the credenza behind Agent Marks. It was opened at just the right angle for her to see that it held the same plaster tableau that Brent and Eddie had carried to the Lincoln Bedroom earlier. Only this one was broken into a few big pieces. It must be the original that the maid broke, Nancy thought.

Marks sat back in his chair and clasped his hands behind his head. "Both of your files are clean," he said. "So tell me, Ms. Drew, what happened in there?"

For the third time Nancy related the few details of the attack.

Marks leaned forward, putting his elbows on his desk. "I'm sure you know it looks a little strange that this statue disappeared the same day you got here, Ms. Drew. Not to mention the fact that you were alone with it in the Diplomatic Reception Room for several minutes."

George sat up and said, "You can't be suggesting that Nancy—"

Marks pointed a finger at George, interrupting her. "You're not above suspicion yourself, young lady."

George was silent.

"It's okay," Nancy said, trying to keep her friend calm. "I understand how it looks, Agent Marks. But I'm telling you the truth."

"For your sake, I hope so." Agent Marks tapped away at the keyboard some more. "Did either of you notice anything suspicious about the way Brent Larson was acting while he was in the room? Was he nervous, jumpy?"

"No," George replied. "He just seemed excited. You know, about getting the pictures taken."

Marks read the screen for a moment, then got a strange look on his face. "This is very interesting." He let his voice trail off. After jotting down some notes, he stood up abruptly and said, "That's it for now."

Nancy motioned to the box of broken plaster behind the Secret Service agent. "I see you've got the mess in the Lincoln Bedroom cleaned up."

Marks glanced behind him in surprise. "Oh, right. At least Larson came through for us on that one. The replacement looks exactly the same."

Marks walked the girls out of the office. "Let me know if you remember anything else," he said. "I don't have to tell you how sensitive this situation is. It could turn into a real embarrassment for the administration, so let us do the investigating. Do you understand, Ms. Drew?" Marks tried to smile at them as they left, but Nancy could tell he wasn't used to being friendly.

The girls headed back to George's cubicle. West Wing staffers were putting on their jackets and coming out of their offices.

"People are getting ready for the second half of the work day," George quipped. "Work from nine to five; socialize from five till whenever."

As George stepped into her cubicle, she felt something crinkle under her foot. "What's that?" she asked.

"It's an envelope," Nancy said, stooping to pick it up. She handed it to George.

George pulled a neatly folded sheet of typing paper from the envelope. Nancy watched as her friend's eyes scanned the page. They first widened, then narrowed.

"What do you make of this?" George asked, handing over the note.

The words were handwritten, in childlike block letters. It read:

A warning from a friend: Ambition cuts down anything in its path.

Ask yourself—who *wasn't* there today? Who *seems* to have the most to lose?

Watch your back, or you'll end up like J.N.

4

Serious Threats

"This note sounds like a threat," Nancy said. "J.N. Could that be Joe Newman, your boss?"

George brought her hand to her mouth. "You think Joe's mugging is connected to what happened this afternoon?"

"It sure sounds that way. Who else was supposed to be at the shoot, George?"

George went to her desk and shoved aside a huge stack of loose papers. She dug around for a moment and came up with a schedule. "I don't know, exactly," she admitted. "Brent mentioned that some of the people from the negotiating teams on both sides would be there. I don't know if that meant that Eddie's father would be there, but I do know that Felicia Bingham was supposed to show up. You know, she's Todd Willis's boss at the National Security Council. She was really in charge of the whole negotiating process."

Nancy carefully folded the note and put it back in its envelope. "I think we should take this person's advice and watch out for each other," she said.

The girls left the same way Nancy had come in earlier in the day. They passed through a metal detector that Nancy hadn't noticed before. The only evidence of it was a slight rise under the carpeting and bulges in the walls and ceiling where the device was set. The young marine saluted them as they exited the West Wing and headed to George's car.

It was around five-thirty P.M., and the summer sun was still beating down. The air was humid and heavy. "Agent Marks seemed awfully interested in Brent Larson," Nancy said, as they settled into George's rented white sedan.

George pulled the car up to the entrance of Ellipse Road, an enormous traffic circle with outlets onto Constitution Avenue and E Street. When she saw a tiny opening in the rush hour traffic, she accelerated and zoomed in between two other cars. Nancy held her breath.

"There are some nasty rumors going around about Brent," George said. Her forehead wrinkled in concentration as she worked her way to the eastbound Constitution Avenue exit. "I heard that his father's auction house is declaring bankruptcy," she continued. "There was some sort of big scandal involving secret auctions of smuggled artwork."

"That could be a motive for stealing the hummingbird," Nancy said. "A piece like that would bring big bucks on the black market, I'm sure."

"I don't know," George said. "Rumors are what make this town run. You can't believe everything you hear, though. You've only been here for a few hours, Nan, and I bet there's stuff going around about you already."

"Okay, George, what have you been saying?"

George laughed for the first time since before the photo shoot. "Just wait till you find out," she joked.

As George drove down Constitution Avenue, they passed one imposing concrete office building after another. Then she rounded the U.S. Capitol building and zipped into a multilevel parking garage. They found a parking space on an upper level, and a few minutes later were back out on the street. It was a short walk to the Madison Hotel.

"Here we are," George announced.

A doorman dressed in an emerald green uniform, complete with cap and gold epaulettes, held the door open for them. Inside, thick Persian carpets muffled the sound of their footsteps and fresh flower arrangements filled the room with the scent of rose and lilac. Several well-dressed men sat in overstuffed chairs, reading newspapers. Nancy imagined they were waiting for their wives to come down the hotel's curving marble staircase, exquisitely dressed for dinners at chic, expensive restaurants.

An elderly man in a black tuxedo with a hotel name tag pinned to his lapel approached them. "Where might I direct you young ladies?"

"We're here for the wild horses fund-raiser," George replied, giving the concierge their names.

The man pulled a list from his inside jacket pocket and consulted it. Brent had been true to his word and gotten them on the guest list.

"Very good," the concierge said. He then led them across the lobby to a crowded reception room. Unlike the sedate lobby, this room was packed with young people and abuzz with lively conversation.

"George, you said that a number of these receptions happen every day. How do people decide which ones to go to?" Nancy asked.

The girls had worked their way into the crowd. George almost had to shout to be heard. "Many of these people go to whatever cause is the most popular at the moment. Today it's wild horses, tomorrow it could be nuclear submarines. Some people just come for the party and to see and be seen."

Nancy and George made their way to the buffet tables at the back of the room. It was there that they saw a small stack of brochures about the plight of the wild horses in South Dakota and Wyoming—right next to the sliced cheese and the vegetable dip.

"Over there," Nancy said, pointing to the end of the long tables. "It's Brent."

"And my favorite person is with him," George said.

"Darcy," Nancy said.

The girls made their way over. Brent brightened immediately when he saw George. Darcy's reaction wasn't quite as positive.

"Well, if it isn't the two friends from River Hicks, oops, I mean River Heights," Darcy said. She laughed at her own joke, then tossed her long hair back over her shoulder. "Just kidding, girls."

Brent winced. He put his plate down and quickly poured George and Nancy cups of punch. "I'm glad you made it," he said to them. He turned back to Darcy. "Will you excuse us for a minute, Darcy?"

She scowled. "Oh, sure. I guess you have a lot of secret West Wing stuff to talk about."

When no one answered her, Darcy made a big production of putting her plate down and going off into the crowd to mingle.

"What did Marks say?" Brent asked as soon as she was gone.

"Not much," Nancy replied. Brent seemed genuinely worried about the missing statue, but if he was somehow involved, she didn't want to give him too much information. "He seems to be doing a thorough investigation," she added.

"Let's hope so," Brent said.

Nancy wondered about the rumors of Brent's family's money problems that George had told her about. "Two hundred dollars is a lot of money, Brent," she told him. "You shouldn't have paid to get us in here."

Brent dismissed her comment with a wave. "Oh, it's no big deal. I'm just happy you made it."

Nancy felt a hand rest gently on her shoulder. She turned to see Eddie Enriquez standing next to her. He wore a khaki-colored linen suit that contrasted with his thick, dark hair. But he had a look of concern on his face.

"Nancy, how are you feeling? Did you see a doctor?" he asked.

Nancy shot a look at Brent, but he was busy talking to George. She and Eddie strolled to a quiet corner of the room. "How did you know about this afternoon?" she asked.

Eddie smiled. "I know Brent was supposed to keep quiet about the statue, but he felt I should know."

"You don't seem too upset about what happened."

"Only about what happened to you." Eddie took an hors d'oeuvre from a passing waiter and offered it to Nancy. "Here, you must try this—a stuffed mushroom."

Nancy accepted and, after eating the hors d'oeuvre, asked, "You aren't concerned about what happened to the hummingbird?"

"As I said, there are many people in my country who think the bird belongs at home. They also tend not to like the idea of an economic agreement with the United States. They think our tiny country will be overrun with hamburger joints and drive-in theaters." Eddie laughed. "They have no idea that drive-in theaters aren't very popular here anymore."

"And who are these people?"

Eddie scanned the room, as if on the lookout for someone. "The most organized group is probably *Los Luchadores del Noche*—the Night Fighters. They've threatened my father's life several times."

Nancy silently wondered whether such a terrorist group could have found its way into the White House. "Since you're a student here in Washington, I take it you're not too afraid of hamburger joints."

Eddie shrugged and said, "I don't agree with all the plans my father and the president of San Valente have. But let's talk about something else," he suggested, "like tomorrow night. My parents are hosting a dinner party at the Kennedy Center. Would you and George do me the honor of being my guests?"

Nancy felt herself beaming. "We'd love to," she answered. "I just hope I brought the right kind of clothes for such an affair."

"I'm sure you'll look gorgeous, no matter what you wear," he said as he led Nancy back over to where Brent and George were standing. He waved goodbye to George and Brent, then briefly clasped Nancy's hands in his. "Meet me at the upper terrace of the Kennedy Center tomorrow—say, around eight o'clock."

"We'll be there."

"Well, Nan," George said, after Eddie had left. "You ready to get out of here? I think somebody's about to make a long, boring speech."

Nancy had spotted a podium being set up at the far end of the room. "I'm ready," she said.

As if sensing that George and Nancy were about to leave, Darcy materialized out of the crowd and

42

placed herself at Brent's elbow. "Now I get you all to myself," she said, giggling.

Nancy saw the look of disappointment in Brent's eyes. "Have fun," she said, winking at him.

As they turned to go, they heard Darcy's high-pitched voice. "Oh, George," she called out. "I almost forgot. I scheduled a shoot for you tomorrow morning at six. The president's dog, Muffin, is having a bath, and the first family wants some shots for the family album."

George stopped in her tracks. "The dog's bath? At six in the morning? You're kidding, right?"

Darcy shook her head back and forth, a smug smile on her face.

Nancy watched her friend strain to control herself. "Thank you, Darcy," George finally managed to say. "I'm sure it'll be great fun."

Outside, the sun had set and the air was much cooler than inside the crowded hotel.

"Six A.M.?" George muttered. "The poor dog won't be awake yet, not to mention me."

Nancy buttoned her blazer and wrapped a light scarf around her neck. "Maybe you should accept Darcy's offer to take over some of the shoots. And let her capture Muffin tomorrow in all her bubbly splendor."

"That's just what Darcy wants. But she's not going to get it."

They quickly found the car inside the crowded parking garage. George switched on the headlights and backed out of the narrow parking space. She carefully navigated down a succession of concrete ramps leading toward street level. As they turned down yet another aisle, Nancy noticed headlights suddenly illuminate their car from behind.

George squinted into the mirror. "Nice way to tailgate me, buddy."

Then the two girls felt the violent jolt of their car being rammed. Glass shattered behind them, and Nancy heard the sound of tearing metal.

"Hey!" George cried. "What's going on?" She wrenched the wheel to stay on course, just barely missing a parked car.

They were still three stories off the ground. Nancy could see the top of the Washington Monument in the distance. George started to slow to a stop when the other car appeared behind them again, quickly closing in.

"Go! Go!" Nancy yelled.

The car smashed into them again. George tried to steer, but the car was out of control and heading straight for the railing—and a thirty-foot drop to the road below.

5

Close Call

"Jump!" Nancy yelled.

George had both feet jammed onto the brakes. The tires burned and squealed against the pavement, but their attacker relentlessly forced them toward the low guardrail.

Nancy saw George take her hands from the wheel and fumble with her seat belt. Reaching over, Nancy unlatched George's buckle, then grabbed for her own door handle.

She dove as far from the car as she could, tumbling along the concrete floor. She heard their car hit the railing and looked up. The other car bore down on her. Nancy ducked her head down as their attacker gunned the engine and roared off, the front tire barely missing her head.

Nancy jumped up. "George?" She couldn't see George, only their car, its front wheels on top of the crushed low railing. The headlights shot beams into the night, three stories over the street.

"George? Where are you? Are you all right?"

Nancy found her friend kneeling on the pavement on the other side of the car.

"I'm okay," George said, standing up. "I can't say the same for my clothes, though." She held up her arm, revealing a long rip in her jacket sleeve. She shuddered, then took a deep breath. "That was close."

"I got a look at the car—a black or dark blue sedan. It had government plates, I think," Nancy said.

"Get any of the numbers?"

"No," Nancy replied. "I couldn't make them out and protect my head at the same time. But whoever it was definitely wanted to put us in the hospital right next to Joe Newman."

"Or worse," George said. "Should we call the police?"

Nancy surveyed George's rental car. The damage wasn't as bad as it could've been. "No," she said. "I think that's just what whoever's behind this wants us to do. A big public investigation will stall the negotiations with San Valente, maybe bring an end to the whole thing."

The girls heard a vehicle coming down from an upper floor of the garage. They watched as headlights panned along the far wall and a car turned down the aisle and came toward them.

When it was clear that this driver wasn't intent on terrorizing them, Nancy stepped out to where she could be seen. "Time to play damsels in distress," she said.

The car came to a stop beside them. "What in the world happened to you all?" Todd Willis stuck his head out the driver's window.

"Hey, Todd. Just a minor navigational problem," Nancy answered. "Can you help us out?"

The young Security Council officer climbed out of his car, his long limbs seeming to unfold as he stood up. He brushed a lock of bushy, chestnut-colored hair out of his eyes and walked around the wrecked car. "This could be considered modern art, you know. You're lucky you weren't killed," he said. "Did this happen just now?"

"You're the first friendly face on the scene," Nancy said.

"So you didn't see Bureau Chief Bingham?" Todd asked, referring to his boss. "We were both parked on the top floor, and she left just before me."

"We must've just missed her," George said. "What kind of car does she drive?"

Willis looked over the car's hood to the street below. "Oh, I don't know," he said. "It's a big black four-door, I think. She gets a government car to tool around in. You know, perks of a power position and all."

Nancy and George exchanged glances. Could Felicia Bingham, architect of the San Valente economic treaty, have tried to kill them?

Todd motioned for George to get in the driver's seat of the rental car. "I think we can get this thing unstuck," he said. "You might still be able to drive it."

George started the engine. She placed her foot on the brakes and put the car in reverse, while Todd raised the front end as best he could.

The car bounced down from the guardrail, and George let off the brake, easing the car back. The engine was running smoothly.

"Thanks," George said out the open window.

Willis grinned. "No problem." He swiped at the lock of hair again. It seemed to have a mind of its own.

Nancy got into the passenger seat while

George made sure all the lights and signals still worked.

Todd leaned down to George's window and looked in. "You guys were at the wild horse thing, I guess."

They both nodded.

"Yeah. That's a good cause," Todd said. "Chief Bingham and I were having dinner with some San Valente delegates." Willis seemed quite proud to be able to talk so casually about meeting with important people.

"That sounds exciting," Nancy said. She wondered if he was just trying to show off.

"Everything's touch and go now that the bird's missing," Todd said. "I had to do some fancy talking tonight to keep everyone off the subject."

"You didn't tell Chief Bingham?" Nancy asked.

"No way," Todd said with a laugh. "She'd go nuts if she found out. I'm the one holding this process together."

"Well, we're still hoping the statue will turn up safe and sound," Nancy said, "so you can finish up the negotiations."

"Yeah, I hope so, too," Todd said. He stepped back from the car. "Be careful on the way home, now."

Nancy thanked Willis again for his help and George drove off to Georgetown.

For young Washingtonians, Georgetown was the place to be. The night-time streets were lined with glowing gaslights, quaint antique shops, and fancy restaurants. College students and congressional staffers stood in line waiting to get into some of the more popular places.

George pulled up in front of an elegant, Federal-style town house, its white facade brightly lit. Though George had been lucky to get such a great place to live, Nancy was too tired to get very excited about it. Once inside George's apartment, she tossed her suitcase on the floor, kicked off her shoes, and flopped down on a comfortable sofa, propping her feet on a glass-top table.

George got a drink of water from the kitchen before sitting down. Picking up the phone, she said, "I'm going to call the hospital and see how Joe's doing."

After being put on hold two or three times, George finally got through to someone who knew something. Nancy noticed the tension in her friend's face disappear as she talked on the phone.

"Good news," George said, hanging up. "Joe's going to be fine. Three or four more days in the hospital, then he can go home."

"That's great. Maybe he can tell us something about who might've attacked him."

"You think whoever mugged Joe is the same maniac who came after us tonight?"

Nancy sat up. "Considering that cryptic note you got, which referred to Joe, I think that a connection is likely."

George had taken off her ripped jacket and was now examining her shoes and skirt for damage. "All we know for sure is that it's someone with access to the White House."

"Right. The person got into the Diplomatic Reception Room to steal the hummingbird and leave the note under your door. Maybe the person who attacked us was making good on that threat."

Nancy took the letter out of its envelope. "Who wasn't at the shoot today and who seems to have the most to lose? Those are the two big questions."

"Eddie's father wasn't there," George said. "As the ambassador from San Valente, he'd have a lot to lose."

"And Todd's boss, Felicia Bingham—she wasn't there either," Nancy noted. "As a chief negotiator, she's got a lot invested in this treaty, too—and she has a dark sedan."

They both sat and thought silently for a minute.

"As much as I hate to believe it, I think we have to consider Eddie a suspect," Nancy said.

"Why? What do you mean?"

"I asked him a few questions at the fund-raiser," Nancy said. "He didn't seem at all concerned about the missing statue."

"You really think he cracked you over the head and then tried to kill us in the parking garage?"

Nancy felt an overwhelming rush of sadness. She realized how much she liked Eddie and wanted him to be innocent. "I don't know if he'd do something like that," she replied. "I don't think so, but I don't know."

"If the rumors about Brent are true," George said, "then he has a pretty good motive as well—money. And he's one of the few people around with the connections to sell the bird on the black market."

"Take your own advice, George. Try not to pay attention to rumors."

George frowned.

"But there's a way to separate rumor from fact," Nancy continued. "I want to get into Agent Marks's office and take a look at those FBI files."

"Good luck," George said doubtfully.

"I also want to have a little talk with your friend Darcy O'Neill. She knew all about the photo shoot of the hummingbird and who was supposed to be there."

George stood up and stretched. 'I don't know

about you, Nan, but I need my beauty sleep. I've got to be up and at the residence by six to shoot Muffin in the bath.''

Nancy laughed. ''Just be sure to wipe all your fingerprints off and don't leave the murder weapon behind.''

George chuckled and threw a pillow at Nancy, who batted it back at her.

''You take your car then, and I'll take a cab over later in the morning,'' Nancy suggested.

George made sure the front door was locked, then showed Nancy her room.

Nancy fell asleep as soon as her head hit the pillow. She dreamed about dancing with Eddie Enriquez in a vast ballroom filled with a hundred other couples.

The next morning Nancy arrived at the West Wing gate dressed in her smartest suit—forest green, with a double-breasted jacket and a short, straight skirt.

She showed the marine guard her laminated White House pass, and he disappeared back into the guard house. While she waited, Nancy watched tourists gather outside the visitors' gate, cameras in hand.

A few minutes later the guard returned, a stern

53

look on his face. He grasped Nancy by her upper arm and led her into the guardhouse.

"We've got a problem here," he said, speaking into an intercom. He turned to face Nancy. "I'm sorry, miss, but this security pass has been reported as stolen."

6

An Internal Investigation

Two Secret Service agents wearing dark suits and glasses quickly appeared at the guard house door. While Nancy watched, the marine guard punched her ID number onto a computer keyboard. Sure enough, the screen scrolled up showing that her pass had been stolen early that morning.

"May I see your driver's license, Miss?" one of the Secret Service agents asked.

Nancy quickly produced both the license and her social security card.

The agent took off his sunglasses and studied the documents. "Looks to me like you're Nancy Drew," he said. "Did you report the card stolen?"

"No."

"Can you think of any reason why someone would think your pass had been lost?"

"No," Nancy replied. "How often do mixups like this happen?"

The marine guard arched his eyebrows and looked at the agents. "I've never had this happen before," he said.

"Let us make some phone calls, Ms. Drew," the second agent said. "Who's your contact inside the White House?"

Nancy gave him George's name and then, for good measure, the name of the White House chief of staff, the man who'd given George the internship.

Nancy took a seat on a plain wooden chair in a corner of the guard house. After a few phone calls, the two Secret Service agents politely apologized for the inconvenience and left. The marine came over and handed Nancy back her pass.

"Someone in the White House Advance Office reported the card stolen," he said. "Now it turns out whoever it was made a mistake. I'm sorry to have held you up."

Nancy immediately thought of Darcy O'Neill in the Advance Office. This was no honest mistake. "It's not your fault," she said to the guard. "You were just doing your job."

The marine tipped his hat to Nancy as she left

the guardhouse. "Thanks for your patience, Ms. Drew."

She didn't let on to the Honor Guard, but Nancy was upset. Instead of entering the West Wing, she passed back through White House security and crossed the street to the Old Executive Office Building. Nancy felt it was time that she and Darcy had a little heart-to-heart chat.

Though the building was enormous, Nancy quickly found Darcy's cubbyhole office. Darcy, however, wasn't there.

Nancy stood in the hallway, determined to get to the bottom of the incident. She spotted a door labeled Janice Paul: Principal Executive Planner of Executive Itinerary and Travel Detail. That sounded like the title of Darcy's supervisor. Nancy started to knock on the door, but decided against it. She wanted to confront Darcy herself.

Nancy started back to the West Wing. She didn't consider Darcy a prime suspect in the theft of the statue anyway. She was just a petty, jealous person, as George had said.

Returning to the West Wing, Nancy thought, How do I find a way to get a look at those FBI files on Don Marks's computer? She hoped the files would reveal something significant about one of her suspects.

Nancy took the stairs to the basement. If anybody asked her what she was doing, she planned to pretend she was lost and ask where George's office was. She headed down the hallway toward Marks's office, passing the dining hall, which echoed with the clatter of dishes. An old man in the navy blue uniform of the White House domestic staff came out of a service closet carrying a mop. He swung it over his shoulder without looking, and Nancy had to duck quickly to avoid a collision. What a morning! she thought.

She walked past Marks's office instead of charging right in. The door was closed, but as she rounded the corner at the end of the hall, she heard it open. Stopping in front of a water fountain, she bowed her head to get a drink.

When Nancy looked up, she saw that Marks's secretary had come out of the office, shutting the door behind her, and was walking off toward the dining room. Nancy remembered that lower-level staff picked up their lunches in the mess hall and brought them back to their own desks. Unless Marks's secretary had other plans, Nancy wouldn't have much time before the young woman returned.

She walked casually back to Marks's office. The doorknob turned smoothly and the door opened quietly. Nancy stepped inside, just as quietly closing the door behind her. The door to Agent

Marks's inner office was open, and there were no sounds of typing, paper shuffling, or telephones ringing. She peered in and was relieved to find it empty.

The box with the shattered replica of the *Neighboring Pews* tableau still sat on the credenza. Nancy noticed that Agent Marks seemed to be trying to glue the fractured pieces of the church scene back together. He had almost figured it out, but whether it would be worth anything again, Nancy couldn't guess.

She sat down at the computer and studied the screen. Marks's word-processing program was open, and he had obviously been working on a secure E-mail message to other Secret Service agents.

Secure Transmission via WH intranet code 451
From: Agent Don Marks, Head of Residence Security
To: Residence Perimeter Posts
Re: Routine Security System Maintenance
   Make note that the perimeter security system, including closed circuit video surveillance and metal detectors, will be down for routine service for approximately one hour tomorrow afternoon between 1:00 and 2:00 P.M. All staff and visitors entering or leaving the premises during that time

will be subject to pat-down search. Be extra vigilant.

Delete this message after reading.

Nancy saved the file and closed it. Finding the security file database, she tried to bring up Brent Larson's file. To Nancy's horror, the screen suddenly went blank. Then, just as she was certain she'd triggered some kind of silent alarm, the screen came back to life. The prompt asked her to enter a password.

She had to think fast. Agent Marks probably changed his password every few weeks. "He'd need something he could remember easily," she murmured to herself. "A rotation of three of four different passwords he could alternate every so often." Glancing around the room, Nancy's eyes fell upon the framed pictures of Agent Marks with the three previous presidents.

"It's worth a try," she whispered. Nancy typed in the last name of the oldest of the ex-presidents. The hard disk whirred, then stopped. Four words popped up on the screen: "Password Incorrect. Try Again." Nancy figured she had one or two more tries before the machine shut her out for good. She carefully typed the name of another ex-president.

"Yes!" Nancy said under her breath. The database opened. Nancy quickly typed in "Larson, Brent."

She scanned the pages. At first, Brent's credentials seemed impeccable. An Ivy League education in art history and restoration. Internships with several top museums. He'd even spent a semester in San Valente, helping to design a national pre-Columbian art exhibit. "No wonder he was so knowledgeable about the hummingbird," Nancy thought.

Then it hit her: What if Brent had made connections with the Night Fighters during his stay in San Valente? He could be working for them now.

The file went downhill from there. The rumors of money and legal problems George had mentioned were all documented in detail in the file. Brent wasn't implicated in any of his father's shady dealings, but it appeared that he had probably been involved—right up to his bright blue eyes.

Nancy next opened Darcy O'Neill's file. Somewhat regretfully, she found nothing incriminating, but she did find something that was missing. George would be happy to hear that Darcy had no previous photography experience listed. She was just faking it, trying to weasel her way into George's job.

Todd Willis's file was clean. Like Brent, he had

spent time in South America, but none of it in San Valente. He'd obviously worked very hard to get to his present position in the National Security Council.

Nancy stopped for a second and listened, but all she heard was the hum of the computer. No sign of the secretary. She typed in "Bingham, Felicia." The screen answered her with: "Access Denied. Secure to Level 9/CIA/NSC."

"Interesting," Nancy mused quietly. Bingham was too powerful for even Agent Marks to touch.

Finally, she punched in Eddie's name. She waited anxiously for the file to open. What would she do with the information she got? How would she feel if she had to turn him in?

The screen came up blank: "No file by that name." Nancy realized she'd been holding her breath. She let it out in a long rush. Instead of considering how odd it was to find nothing at all on Eddie—who had a security pass like the rest of them—Nancy told herself that this was a case of no news equals good news.

As she closed the database, she caught a whiff of something in the air. It was the smell of fried rice and egg rolls. The secretary, Nancy thought, her heart thumping. She's back.

Nancy quietly and quickly reopened the E-mail letter that had originally been on the screen.

When it reappeared, she stood up and went to the office door. She cracked it an inch and peeked through.

Yes. There was Marks's secretary right outside, sitting down at her desk with a plate of food.

There were no windows, no other doors. Nancy was trapped.

7

Poisoned!

Nancy knew she couldn't hesitate. She'd done enough acting, both on the high school stage and in real life, to carry her through. She stepped boldly into the outer office.

"Oh, maybe you could help me," Nancy said as innocently as possible. She extended her hand to the secretary. "Remember me from yesterday afternoon? I'm Nancy Drew, from River Heights."

She'd caught the woman with a mouthful of fried rice. The secretary held her napkin to her mouth and mumbled, "Um-hm."

Before the woman could swallow and ask her any questions, Nancy launched into her story. "Agent Marks asked me to come back and answer some more questions. He said he'd be here at eleven." Nancy looked at her watch. "The door was open, so I thought I'd just come on in and wait in his office. Will he be back soon, do you think?"

The secretary shook her head, not having swallowed yet.

"No? Well, there must've been some kind of misunderstanding then." Nancy waved at the woman and went for the door. "I'll just come back later, okay? Nice talking to you."

With that, she was out in hall. Nancy didn't waste any time. She hurried around the corner to George's cubicle.

George wasn't there, so Nancy decided to track down Todd Willis. He was enough of an insider in the negotiating process to be able to answer some questions she had. If the note George had received was, in fact, from someone involved in the deliberations, maybe Todd could give her some likely names to investigate. He might even know something about Brent Larson's travels in South America.

She found the National Security Council offices on the third floor of the Old Executive Office Building. Unlike Darcy's office, or even the offices of the West Wing, the National Security Council's suite was enormous and sumptuously decorated.

She entered a carpeted reception area through

nine-foot mahogany double doors carved with an intricate scrollwork of flowers and vines. The receptionist directed her to Todd's office, and Nancy found him sitting behind his desk, studying some kind of chart.

"Good morning, Todd."

Todd looked up. "Oh, hi," he said, smiling. "Ms. Drew, right?"

"Right. But please, call me Nancy. May I sit down for a second?"

As if just remembering his manners, Todd stood up and gestured for Nancy to sit in one of the chairs in front of his desk. "Of course. Make yourself comfortable."

Nancy looked around, impressed. Todd's office even had a special alcove on one side arranged like a living room, complete with couch, coffee table, and silver tea service. A framed portrait of Abraham Lincoln hung prominently on the wall behind Todd's desk.

"I just wanted to come by and thank you again for all your help last night," Nancy said. "I don't think George and I ever would have gotten our car off that railing without you."

"How'd you get into that situation in the first place?"

Nancy laughed. "You know, I couldn't even tell

you. One minute we're having this great conversation, the next we're barreling toward the guardrail." She hated sounding so featherbrained, but she wasn't going to let the story out until she had some idea of who was behind it.

Todd just shook his head in disbelief.

Nancy's eye caught the chart Todd had been looking at when she came in. "And I'm so interested in what goes on here, I just wondered if I could ask you a few questions," she continued.

"Oh, sure thing," Todd said with a smile. "Shoot."

Good work, Nancy told herself. He's warming up. "What is that?" She pointed to the paper on his desk. "The seating chart for the state dinner tomorrow night?"

Todd stuck the paper under a stack of manila folders. "No way. We leave all that tedious work for the drones in the Advance Office."

"What's it like to work with Felicia Bingham?" Nancy asked.

"Work with? Work *for* is more like it." Todd snapped the cap to his fountain pen on and off. "For the past year, I've been taking care of every aspect of these negotiations. I do the research, write the proposals, get people together, everything. I barely get any thanks for it."

Nancy could tell she'd touched a nerve. "Do you mean that Bureau Chief Bingham doesn't care if this agreement gets signed?"

Todd held his hands up as if protecting himself from an attacker. "Whoa! I didn't say that. Chief Bingham's career rides on the success of this San Valente deal. If it goes down, she goes down." Todd leaned forward, whispering now. "That's why it's so important to me that we get that statue back before tomorrow. If the president of San Valente figures out we lost a priceless gift he gave us, well, it's all over."

Nancy remembered the specific wording of George's note—"Who seems to have the most to lose?" It didn't make sense. If Bingham had everything to lose, why would she sabotage the negotiations?

Nancy decided to take a chance and confide in Todd. "Don Marks seems to think Brent Larson had a good motive to steal the bird."

Todd frowned and sat back in his leather chair. "That's how rumors get started," he said.

"You and Brent are friends?"

"No. He thinks he knows a lot about South American foreign policy because he spent some time down there as an art student, but other than that I don't know much about him. If I've heard

68

some things going around about his father's auction house, I've tried not to repeat them. I am not a fan of gossip."

"What about Eddie Enriquez?"

"What is this, twenty questions?"

Nancy smiled and backed off. "I'm just really impressed that someone your age could have so much responsibility," she said, pouring on the charm. "It must be a nightmare trying to get all these different personalities together to agree on something."

It worked. Todd seemed to relax again.

"You don't know the half of it. Eddie's father, Ambassador Enriquez, keeps on changing the times of the meetings. He's very difficult to pin down. Todd let out a big sigh, as if just thinking about it all made him tired. "It's crazy. And Eddie hasn't helped matters at all."

"How do you mean?"

"It's hard to explain. He keeps butting in, making suggestions. It's like he wants the best of both worlds. He wants San Valente to stay this isolated little place with all its cute little traditions, but he also acts like it should try to become some kind of economic powerhouse—a place overflowing with appliance stores and car dealerships."

"Yeah, he told me about this group, the Night Fighters," Nancy said. "He says they threatened his father. Is that true?"

"Mr. Willis?" A woman's voice interrupted them. "Todd, I'm waiting for that seating chart. I've got to fax that over to the Advance Office before noon today."

Nancy marveled at the voice. It was rich and resonant, like a jazz singer's. Then the owner of the voice came into the office.

Todd stood up, clearly embarrassed that Nancy now knew what he'd really been working on and that he'd lied about it. He recovered quickly, though, and made the introductions. "Nancy Drew, please meet South American Bureau Chief Bingham."

As they shook hands, Nancy recognized the woman from the jumbo print outside George's office. Chief Bingham was the tall, elegantly dressed woman in the picture who was holding the box of fountain pens for the president while he signed an important treaty.

Chief Bingham looked at Nancy as if she recognized her. "I feel like I've seen you before. Have we met?"

"I don't think so," Nancy replied. "Unless it was in the parking garage next to the Madison Hotel last night. Were you there?"

"Yes, just to park my car of course. But that's not where I saw you. I must be mistaken."

The bureau chief turned away from Nancy as if dismissing her. "Listen, Todd. I've got a whole list of things here we need to get done before tomorrow. Can I count on you to handle it?"

"Absolutely."

"Good. Get to it then. Call me if you have any problems." Without acknowledging Nancy, Chief Bingham wheeled around and strode purposefully from the office.

Todd straightened the piles of folders and papers on his desk. "Sorry about that. We're all under a lot of stress here."

"I understand," Nancy said. "Hey, thanks again for your help."

"Any time."

Nancy left Todd's office feeling more confused that ever. Brent and Eddie both seemed to have strong motives to steal the hummingbird. For Brent, it would help his father with his failing business. For Eddie, the disappearance of the bird would shut down the negotiations, or at least postpone them, giving him—and probably the Night Fighters—time to put together their own agenda for their country. She didn't want to believe any of this, but the more she searched, the guiltier they looked.

The one thing Nancy couldn't make sense of was how Chief Bingham fit in. The note and the incident in the parking garage both could have been Bingham's work. But what was her motive?

Walking back to George's office in the West Wing, Nancy's mind drifted to the evening ahead of her—dinner with Eddie at the Kennedy Center. Thinking about it put a light step in her walk. But then, what if it was Eddie who'd smashed into George's car in the parking garage? Nancy remembered that he'd left the fund-raiser just before she and George had. He easily could have been waiting for them.

Nancy felt sad to be suspicious of Eddie. The only thing to do, she decided, was to go to the dinner and follow the advice in George's anonymous note: watch her back.

It was just after noon, and the lunchtime activity in the West Wing was so intense that Nancy had to keep alert just to get safely to George's cubicle. Staffers hustled in and out of offices, ran across the hall for copies. Nancy saw several people typing at keyboards, talking on the phone, and eating sandwiches all at once. Everyone seemed to have some top-priority task to get done before the state dinner the following night.

She found George in her office, slouched at her desk, eyes glazed with exhaustion.

"How was your morning, Fayne?" Nancy slapped her hand on the desk to rouse her friend.

George lifted one dark eyebrow and peered at her friend dubiously. Then she silently pointed to big, wet stains on her silk blouse. "I spent the entire morning chasing a wet cocker spaniel around the rose garden, which, by the way, is filled with tulips, not roses."

Laughing, Nancy placed a chair next to George and sat down. "Did you get some good shots?"

"Oh, just great," George said. "Muffin splashing me, Muffin running away, cute little Muffin rolling around in a big pile of dirt." George pointed to a plate on the desk. Half a sandwich sat among some crumbs. "By the way, Nan, thanks for getting me lunch. That was nice of you."

"What? I didn't get that for you."

George looked puzzled. "But the note's right here." She picked up a scrap of paper and read aloud: "'G. Here's something to keep you going. See you soon. Love, Nan.'"

"I didn't write that, George."

"That's strange." George sat up straight, putting her hand on her stomach. "I left my office door open so you could get in if you needed to."

"Someone else was in here," Nancy said in a low voice. She and George locked eyes for a tense moment.

73

"All of a sudden I don't feel so good," George said.

"George—you're as pale as a ghost!" Nancy exclaimed. Her friend looked as if she was breaking into a cold sweat.

George doubled over in pain.

"George! What's happening?"

"I think I just need to lie down," George said. With Nancy at her arm, she stood up. "I'll just go to the lounge for a minute." George's voice sounded sleepy and far away. She took a couple of halting steps toward the hallway.

Nancy watched in horror as George's knees suddenly buckled and she collapsed to the floor.

8

The Stranger in the Darkness

"George, George!" Nancy cried. "You only ate half of that sandwich, right?"

George's voice was a mere whisper. "Nan, it was the food."

"It must have been poisoned!" Nancy exclaimed. She leaped up and shouted down the hallway for help. Three or four people rushed in.

"George is sick," Nancy said. She took off her jacket and wrapped it around George as best she could. "Is there an infirmary in the building?"

A slight young man with wire-rim glasses picked up the phone on George's desk. "There's always a doctor on call here," he said, already dialing the number.

Nancy knelt down next to George while they all waited anxiously. Her breathing seemed steady and strong, but she was pale and shivering violently. Nancy held on to her shoulders to comfort her.

"Okay, clear out now!" The voice came from outside in the hall. "Let's have some room, some air in here!" A trim, middle-aged woman wearing a white lab coat over a business suit pushed through the crowd at the door. She knelt down next to George and briskly opened her medical bag. "What happened here?" the woman asked.

Nancy noticed that everything about the doctor was neatly organized, from the row of pens in her breast pocket to the instruments in her bag.

"Something she ate made her sick," Nancy said.

The doctor took George's blood pressure and pulse, then pushed gently around her abdomen. "What did she have for lunch?"

Nancy retrieved the half-eaten sandwich from George's desk and handed it to the doctor.

The doctor unfolded a pair of gold-rimmed glasses and put them on. She peeled off the top piece of bread. It looked like a regular turkey and Swiss cheese sandwich to Nancy. The cheese was covered with little sproutlike greens.

The doctor pinched off one of the sprouts and smelled it.

"What is it?" Nancy asked.

"I think it's ipecac," the doctor said, taking a tiny taste.

"Ipecac?" Nancy asked. "As in syrup of ipecac that makes you throw up?"

"Exactly. Has she vomited?"

"No," Nancy said.

"Then it probably wasn't a severe does," the doctor said, to Nancy's relief. "It's a good thing she didn't eat the whole sandwich."

The doctor put the sandwich down and spoke softly to George. "You're going to be just fine, honey. We'll take you to the infirmary where you can rest this afternoon. You'll be feeling just like yourself by tonight."

George could only nod gratefully.

A nurse soon arrived with a gurney, and while she and several others got George ready to go, Nancy drew the doctor aside.

"What exactly is ipecac?"

"It's a plant," the doctor replied. "Actually the dried root of a plant. It contains emetine, which taken in large enough doses can make you violently ill or even kill you."

"Does that mean someone deliberately tried to hurt George?" Nancy asked.

The doctor folded her glasses and put them away. "There isn't enough in this sandwich to do serious harm," she said. "But this is just about the meanest practical joke I've ever seen."

"Where would someone get that stuff?"

"The plant comes from South America, I believe, but you can get the seeds here and sprout them." The nurse started to roll George out of the office. "Excuse me, honey," the doctor said to Nancy. "I've got to tend to my patient."

Nancy followed along, deep in thought. Was it just a coincidence that ipecac came from South America? And why would someone target George? If a person wanted to disrupt the trade negotiations, then why poison a photographer's assistant?

George still looked awfully ill when Nancy met her in the infirmary in the Old Executive Office Building. Before George could get settled into a bed to rest, Brent showed up, concern showing on his face.

"I heard you were sick," he said, sitting on a stool next to George's bed. "How are you feeling?"

George glared at Nancy. "I can't believe you let him in here. How could you let him see me like this?"

Nancy laughed. "I can see you're feeling better already."

Brent took George's hand. "You're so cold," he said. "What happened?"

"I don't know. One minute I felt fine, then the next I almost passed out."

They stayed with George until she drifted off to sleep. Then Nancy asked Brent if he wanted to get some lunch somewhere outside the White House.

"We need to talk about what happened to George," she added.

"Sure. We'll take my car over to Georgetown."

Brent, it turned out, drove a red convertible. Nancy was thankful it wasn't a black sedan with dents in the front end—that would've been too much to handle at that moment.

It was a perfect day, so Brent lowered the top and they sped off down Pennsylvania Avenue toward Washington Circle. The breeze blew Nancy's long hair back, and she tucked a few stray strands behind her ear.

"George was poisoned," she said, suddenly.

Brent turned to look at her, his mouth open in surprise. Nancy couldn't see his eyes behind his sunglasses, but she was satisfied that his reaction was genuine. He hadn't known.

"Are you serious?" he asked. "Who would do something like that?"

"That's what I have to find out," Nancy said.

Brent pulled his sports car into a space in front of a fancy little café called the Monocle.

"Too bad George is sick," Nancy said as a

waiter seated them in a private booth by the window. "She would love this place."

"I'll have to bring her here when she's feeling better," Brent said. "You should try the crab cakes. They're amazing."

"I think I'll have the crab salad instead. And a glass of iced tea."

After they ordered, Brent leaned forward, putting his elbows on the table. "Do you think this latest incident with George is connected to the theft?"

"I don't know," Nancy said. "I can't see how everything fits together, can you? But, what else could it be?"

Brent gazed out the window in thought, then turned back to her and took a sip of his tea. "I can't figure it out either. I've been talking with some contacts I have asking them to keep their eye out for the hummingbird, although it's a little early to put it on the market. If I were the person who stole it, I'd hold on to it for a while, let things calm down."

Nancy thought of the rumors going around about Brent. "What kind of contacts do you mean?"

Brent almost choked on a piece of ice. "You've heard what people are saying about me, haven't you?" he asked defensively. "You wouldn't ask that unless you had."

Nancy knew she'd overplayed her hand, but all she could do was follow up on what she'd started. "Listen, Brent. Someone tried to run George and me off the top of a parking garage last night. I'm just trying to figure out who's behind all this."

Again, Brent wore a look of astonishment. "Run you off . . . ? When? After the fund-raiser? Did you call the police?"

Nancy put out her hands, signaling Brent to tone it down. She related the story about being hit from behind by a dark-colored sedan. "We didn't call the police because we didn't want to deal with questions and publicity," Nancy said. "I thought about telling Agent Marks, but there's nothing he could do about it. He doesn't have jurisdiction there. Besides, he's got his hands full looking for the statue."

"Yeah," Brent said bitterly. "He called me into his office early this morning to ask me a bunch of questions, so don't feel too bad. You're not the only one who thinks I had something to do with the bird disappearing."

"I don't know what to think yet."

"You've got to let me help, Nancy. I'm involved with this, too," Brent said. "Agent Marks says they've been through the entire White House with a fine-tooth comb. They haven't found one clue. So it's up to us. We've got to figure this out—together."

Nancy wanted more than anything to trust Brent. She stayed quiet, letting him continue.

"You know I wasn't driving that car last night," Brent said. "Because you and George abandoned me with Darcy O'Neill. While someone was playing bumper cars with you guys, I was being bored to death back in the hotel."

"Yes, that's true," Nancy admitted. But, she thought to herself, that didn't mean Brent wasn't working with someone else—with Eddie, even.

The waiter brought their food. Nancy's salad looked delicious, but she didn't have much of an appetite. She picked at it with her fork.

"How long have you known Eddie?" she asked.

"I don't know, three or four years, maybe. I met him when I did an internship in San Valente during college." Brent smiled. "He's a great guy."

"He seems like a tough person to get to know," Nancy said.

Brent took a bite of his crab cake. "Eddie's been kind of preoccupied lately. He's got a lot of stuff to deal with. He's trying to decide if he wants to go back and work in San Valente, or if he's going to stay in Washington and pursue a diplomatic career like his father. It's tough for him."

"I asked him how he felt about the trade agreement, and he wouldn't give me a direct answer."

"Oh," Brent said, dropping his fork to his plate and sitting back. "So now you're implying that Eddie's involved too. Maybe we planned it together. Did you think of that?"

"I have to admit that, yes, the idea did occur to me."

"What can I say to change your mind? Anything?"

Nancy paused, taking a sip of iced tea. She didn't want to upset Brent, but she had to be honest with him. "No," she said, finally. "There's nothing you can say. Solid proof is the only thing that will convince me."

"Fine, I'll have to prove it to you then. I'm telling you now, though, Eddie and I didn't have anything to do with this."

Nancy tried to back off the subject, but it was too late. All their small talk about politics and sports fell flat. Nancy's accusations hung in the air between them, spoiling their lunch.

Nancy insisted on paying the bill. Brent protested but in the end lost the battle. After that, they didn't speak to each other until Brent parked the car back at the White House.

"Are you going to go check on George?" he asked.

Nancy nodded.

"Tell her hello for me, okay? I've got some stuff I have to do, but I'll come by and visit her later this afternoon."

Nancy promised to deliver the message, then they split up. Brent headed toward the West Wing, while Nancy entered the Old Executive Office Building. She felt terrible about accusing Brent. Really, though, she hadn't accused him. She'd merely asked questions that had to be asked. Nancy realized she had hurt his feelings, but that hadn't been her intention.

George was still sleeping peacefully, so Nancy headed back to the West Wing. She needed some quiet time to sit and think. She let herself into George's cubicle and closed and locked the door behind her. Then, taking out a sheet of paper, she started making a list.

She'd gotten as far as "Joe Newman—mugged in Georgetown," when she thought she heard someone out in the hallway.

Nancy glanced up. Through the door's frosted glass window she could see the shifting shadows of someone standing right outside. At first, she didn't pay any attention. Staffers often seemed to gather in the halls to talk.

But she didn't hear any conversation outside. The shadows moved again. Then Nancy saw the doorknob move—someone was trying to get in.

The movement stopped as the person outside realized the door was locked.

Nancy stood up just as a letter came skidding in under the door. She rushed over, picked up the envelope, and tore it open. There it was—the same childlike block lettering from the first note.

"Who's out there?" Nancy yelled.

The shadows on the other side of the door disappeared, and Nancy heard footsteps running down the hall.

Without thinking, she flew out the door.

9

A Suspect Confesses

When Nancy burst into the hallway, it was empty, but she could hear footsteps retreating down the adjoining hall to her left. She took off.

As she rounded the corner, a man stepped out of an office right into her path. Nancy nimbly jumped to the side.

"Watch out!" he shouted.

Nancy just missed him. She could see that the fire door at the end of the hall was slowly swinging closed. Whoever it was must have gone upstairs. Nancy reached the stairwell in seconds. Sensing she was gaining on the letter writer, she took the steps three at a time.

Approaching the second-floor landing, she

could hear the person just ahead of her, going up the next flight. Instinctively, Nancy reached up through the railing spindles, trying to catch an ankle as the person went by. Something struck her hand. She heard the person fall, hands and knees smacking on the cold marble.

At the landing, Nancy stopped, ready to nail the person with a judo toss, if necessary.

But it wasn't necessary.

"Darcy?" Nancy exclaimed.

Sure enough, it was petite, prim Darcy. She crouched on the steps, holding her left knee and rocking in pain.

Nancy helped her down to the landing. Darcy didn't struggle. In fact, under Nancy's stern gaze, Darcy's lower lip started to quiver, as if she might burst into sobs at any moment.

"Do you want to answer questions here in the stairwell, where anyone might hear us? Or would you like to go back to George's office?" Nancy said.

Darcy's thin voice quavered. "I think I can walk. Please, give me just one minute. Then I'll go back with you."

Five minutes later Darcy was seated at George's desk, while Nancy stood before her, note in hand. She read aloud the note Darcy had just delivered.

" 'You had your warning. Ask yourself—what

are my real talents? Who is more deserving? Leave now, or end up like Joe.'"

Nancy looked down at Darcy, who was sobbing pitifully in the chair. This was no terrorist ringleader.

"Darcy, did you write this note?" Nancy asked.

Darcy looked up, tears silently streaking down her cheeks. "What are you talking about?"

"This note and the first one, the one that said 'watch your back.' Who wrote them?"

Darcy dabbed at her face with the sleeve of her blouse. "Nobody," she whined.

"What do you mean, nobody? Should we just take this note to the Secret Service?"

"No! Don't do that. Nobody else wrote the note. I wrote it myself."

"Okay, I'll buy that—it doesn't sound like a professional job. But do you expect me to believe that you mugged Joe Newman?"

Darcy let out a long, mournful sob. "No. No, I could never do that. I only wrote that to get George to quit, that's all."

Now Nancy was really confused. "What do you mean?" She handed Darcy a tissue.

"I just wanted to work in the photographer's office," Darcy said, wiping her eyes. "I applied for the job three times—and then they gave it to *her*.

I couldn't believe it. When Joe got mugged, I decided to use that to scare George. I wanted her to think whoever had hurt Joe was going to come after her, so I wrote that first note."

"And then what did you do?"

Darcy tried to compose herself. "I scheduled the six A.M. shoot with Muffin." She checked to see how her bruised knee was doing, then crossed her arms. "When that didn't work, I sneaked in here and left a sandwich with ipecac root on it."

Nancy thought for a moment. "What time did you leave the fund-raiser last night? Did you leave when George and I did?"

Darcy shook her head. "I didn't leave until after nine o'clock."

"What were you going to do if this didn't work?" Nancy asked, waving the second note in the air. "Bake George some arsenic cookies?"

Darcy looked horrified. "That note was the last thing, I promise. I knew the ipecac was too mean, and I came over here earlier to try to get it back, but George was already sick."

Nancy sat on the edge of George's desk. If what Darcy said was true, that meant the first note had nothing to do with the economic negotiations or the disappearance of the gold hummingbird. It was just a case of West Wing envy after all.

"What are you going to do now?" Darcy asked.

"I'm going to leave that up to George."

Darcy melted into sobs again. "I feel so awful. I can't believe I did those things."

Nancy stood up, went to the door, and held it open. "Go on, Darcy. I'll tell George what happened."

As Darcy slunk past her, Nancy couldn't help adding, "George loves chocolate. She might enjoy a three-pound box of your sincerest apologies."

By the time Nancy got back to the infirmary, it well after five o'clock. George was sitting on the edge of a bed, talking to the nurse.

"You look about a thousand times better," Nancy said.

"Thanks, Nan." George pointed to a bright arrangement of fat, red roses in full bloom. "Did you see what Brent sent me? They're bigger than softballs."

"They're beautiful. Come on, I'll carry them for you. We've got less than three hours to get ready for dinner at the Kennedy Center."

George winked at Nancy. "Not enough time, huh?"

"I need every minute I can get," Nancy said, laughing.

They made their way through the parking lot to

George's beaten-up rental car and headed through rush hour traffic back to Georgetown.

"Brent came by to see me this afternoon," George said. "After he sent the flowers."

Nancy expected George to mention the accusations she'd made against Brent at lunch, but that wasn't what she had to say.

"He can't come to the dinner tonight," George continued. "He said something unavoidable came up with work."

"Oh, I'm sorry," Nancy said. "You can hang on my arm tonight."

"One for Eddie, one for me?"

"Right."

George smiled. "Thanks, girlfriend."

As they neared the town house, they couldn't miss seeing the three-pound box of chocolates sitting on the stoop. It was wrapped in shiny blue foil, with a dozen helium-filled balloons floating above it.

"What's all this?" George asked, batting the balloons around. "There's no card."

"Thank goodness," Nancy said, thinking that Darcy certainly hadn't wasted any time. Once inside, she filled George in on the afternoon's adventure.

George sat stunned.

"Are you okay?" Nancy asked.

"Yeah," George finally replied. "But I don't know whether to strangle her or just laugh. I guess I'm sort of relieved, actually. I'd rather have Darcy after me than some professional terrorist."

"I told her you'd deal with her later," Nancy said. "Meantime, we have a party to go to."

The brass clock on the fireplace mantel read 7:45 when Nancy and George were back downstairs, dressed for dinner.

Nancy affected the pose of a Southern belle, her hand holding an invisible parasol over her head. "Our carriage awaits, Miss Fayne," she drawled.

The two young women painted a stunning picture as they emerged onto the dimly lit street. Nancy wore a long, black halter-top dress. The glowing, antique street lamps accented the red highlights in her hair. George was sheathed in dark green satin, with a tailored white satin collar.

As they climbed into the backseat of the taxi, George told the driver, "The Kennedy Center, please."

Twenty minutes later the cab pulled up in front of an enormous monolith perched high on a hill above the river. A blaze of spotlights turned its exterior walls the color of pearls. A doorman opened the cab door, and George and Nancy stepped out into the lights. After climbing a flight of steps, they entered a cavernous, mirrored hall where colorful flags from at least a hundred countries hung from the cathedral ceilings.

They were escorted across a sea of red carpet to a private elevator that took them directly to the terrace level. As the door hissed open, an usher in a rich red jacket greeted them.

"The ambassador awaits your arrival," he said, with great formality.

Nancy smiled at George and whispered, "Is this for real?"

Eddie greeted them with a broad grin when they stepped out onto the terrace. "You both look fantastic," he said, offering an arm to each.

Nancy returned the compliment. Eddie wore a black tuxedo with a black satin cummerbund and matching bow tie.

She heard him duck down and say to George, "Brent sends his regrets. He says he'll make it up to you."

Eddie led the girls over to a handsome older couple engaged in conversation.

"Mom, Dad," he said. "I'd like you to meet Nancy Drew and George Fayne."

Eddie's parents made the girls feel immediately welcome and at ease.

"We want this to be a relaxed, social dinner," Eddie's mother said. "Just close friends and those who have worked especially hard on the negotiations."

"I've tried to make it clear," the ambassador continued, "we are all here to have fun and simply enjoy each other's company. Business is not the topic of the evening."

"That's a lot to ask in this town," George said.

The ambassador laughed. "I enjoy a challenge, Ms. Fayne. Come, it's time for dinner. You and Nancy are seated with us."

On the way to the table, Nancy gazed around at the other guests. She spotted several people she recognized, including Todd Willis and Bureau Chief Bingham.

The food was amazing, equaled only by the spectacular view of the river and, across the way, the Theodore Roosevelt Memorial all lit up for the night. No one mentioned the negotiations. No one mentioned the priceless missing artifact and impending national embarrassment. Nancy glanced over at Todd and Chief Bingham several times. They looked as if they hadn't a care in the world.

But Nancy couldn't help thinking about the case. She wondered where Brent had to be that was so important. And she worried about Eddie.

Why had he left the shoot of the hummingbird so abruptly? Was he involved in the theft? If so, how could he be so carefree—unless things were going exactly as he'd planned?

As the waiters cleared the dessert dishes away, an orchestra began to tune their instruments. A few minutes later, a melodic slow waltz filled the air.

Eddie turned toward Nancy. "Would you care to dance?"

Nancy offered her hand and allowed Eddie to lead her to the dance floor. Eddie guided her effortlessly across the polished floor. Nancy was enjoying herself so much that she forgot all about the case for the duration of the song.

The waltz ended after what seemed like only a few seconds. A few people clapped, and Eddie leaned close to Nancy's ear. "We have two choices," he said softly. "We can wait for this stodgy band to play some really hot South American dance music, or we can take a midnight tour of the city."

"How long do you think it'll be before the orchestra heats up?"

"A few years, anyway," Eddie said with a smile.

"Then I choose the tour," Nancy replied. "Let me check in with George first, though."

"Get going," George said, when Nancy told her the plan. "Have a good time. I can catch a cab home."

Eddie's father, who had overheard their exchange, interrupted. "Nonsense," he said. "My wife and I will give you a ride, George. Stay here with us and dance."

"I accept," George said, beaming.

"Thank you for a wonderful evening," Nancy said, shaking hands with Mr. and Mrs. Enriquez.

"It was our pleasure," the ambassador said.

Eddie said good night to his parents. Then he and Nancy headed through the atrium, down the elevator, and back to the entrance.

Five or six long, black limousines lined the front drive, and Eddie escorted Nancy up to the third one in line. A muscular man with a thick mustache and a chauffeur's cap leaned against the hood, reading a book by the light of the street lamps.

"Evening, Eduardo," the man said, standing up.

"Good evening, Omar. This is my friend, Ms. Nancy Drew."

Omar tipped his cap to Nancy. "Where to, Eddie?"

"A tour of the city." Eddie looked at Nancy. "How about the Washington Monument first?"

"Sounds perfect."

Omar started to come around the car, but Eddie

held him off with an almost invisible gesture. "I've got it." He opened the door to let Nancy in.

Omar pulled smoothly out onto the Rock Creek Parkway and headed east toward the Mall.

"Your own private limo?" Nancy asked.

Eddie looked sheepish. "The San Valente embassy has a few cars. I try not to make a big deal about it. Have I embarrassed you?"

"Oh, no." Nancy paused. "You and Omar seem to be more like friends than chauffeur and dignitary."

"Omar and I have known each other for years," Eddie said. "He's worked for my father for a long time."

They sat quietly for a few minutes, watching the river and the passing lights of the city.

"I'd like to see the view from the top of the monument," Nancy said. "Do you think it's still open this late?"

When Eddie pulled back the sleeve of his jacket to read his watch, Nancy saw it. It was small, barely noticeable in the dim light, but it was there, on the side of his wrist: a dark tattoo the size of a quarter.

A chill went through Nancy's body as she studied it. The marking was a perfect silhouette of a man's crouching shadow with the letters *LN* beneath it.

She touched the tattoo lightly with her index finger.

Eddie pulled back, as if she'd shocked him. He yanked his sleeve back over the mark.

"That's the sign for *Los Luchadores del Noche*, isn't it?" Nancy said. "Are you a member of the Night Fighters?"

10

The Masked Gunman

"I can explain," Eddie said. "If you'll just hear me out. I was very young, just a teenager, when I joined the gang. But as I got older, I saw how foolish their ways were."

"So," Nancy said cautiously, "you don't belong to the Night Fighters anymore?"

"Here," Eddie said, pulling up his sleeve. "Take a good look. It's not so scary. I've gotten so used to it that I sometimes forget it's there."

Nancy let her fingers touch the tattoo lightly. Eddie's openness about it did nothing to allay her fears. She was riding through Washington at night with a man who might possibly be a member of a terrorist organization and his chauffeur, or body-guard, perhaps.

"I should've told you earlier, Nancy. I just didn't know what you'd think."

"Does your father know?"

Eddie nodded. "He didn't speak to me for weeks after he found out. In fact, that was one of the reasons he accepted the position as ambassador to the United States. He wanted to get me out of the country, away from the rebels."

Nancy watched the back of Omar's head. If he was listening to their conversation, he didn't show it. She quickly decided the best thing to do was to pretend to believe Eddie's explanation, even if she really didn't.

"It just caught me by surprise," she said. "With the statue being stolen and all."

"It's very important that we find *El Pajaro*," Eddie said.

"*El Pajaro?*" Nancy asked.

"Yes, that is what we call the gold hummingbird in San Valente."

"Eduardo." Omar's voice filled the limo—calm, but demanding attention.

"What is it?" Eddie asked.

"I think we're being followed. There's a black four-door sedan two cars behind us. Been there for miles now."

"Don't worry," Eddie said. "This happens a lot. People follow the limousine hoping that some famous rock star will suddenly get out and start signing autographs. They're always disappointed when they see me."

"I don't see what could be disappointing about that," Nancy teased. But she remembered the dark sedan from the night before. Could Eddie be working for the rebels?

Eddie laughed. "I'm glad you can joke. That must mean you aren't *too* afraid of me."

Nancy smiled back, concealing her true feelings. Not only was she being driven along the expressway at sixty miles an hour with a man who might be a terrorist, but now they were being followed as well.

"Would you like me to take you home?" Eddie said, as if reading her thoughts. "I don't want you to be here if you don't trust me."

Nancy glanced out the rear window. "No," she said. "This night has been great so far. Let's do the tour."

"Good," Eddie said, giving her hand a reassuring squeeze. "That's what I wanted to hear."

Omar looked at them in the rearview mirror. "The guy's gone now. Sorry about the false alarm."

Eddie nodded, as if to say it was okay.

A few minutes later, Omar swung the limo to the curb. Eddie held the door open for Nancy, and when she got out she saw the Washington Monument less than a hundred yards away. The lighting caused the base of the giant obelisk to radiate a brilliant yellow. The illumination faded toward the top of the monument, making it look as though it pierced the dark fabric of the night sky.

Eddie put his arm lightly around Nancy's waist and led her toward the elevator on one wall of the monument.

A guard greeted them. "Looks like you're the last visitors of the night." He held the doors open for them.

When the doors closed, Nancy realized that she and Eddie were completely alone. Her heart pounded as the elevator cab rose for what seemed like forever.

The view from the top of the monument turned out to be incredible. "You can see for miles," Nancy said, in little more than a whisper.

Off in the distance, lightning flashed. "Look," Eddie said. "There's a storm moving this way."

"Oh, too bad. There were so many stars earlier this evening," Nancy said.

Eddie pointed out the observation window to the Lincoln Memorial at the other end of the Mall. "Let's see if we can make it there before the rain."

They reentered the elevator and could hear the rumblings of thunder as the doors closed and the elevator began its long drop down to the ground. As they stepped out into the open, a warm, light rain started to fall. "We can stop now, if you wish," Eddie suggested. "Go back to the car and stay dry."

"No way," Nancy said, looking up to the sky and letting the raindrops tickle her face. "We've got this whole place to ourselves, and the rain feels great, don't you think?" She felt safe with Eddie as long as they were around guards. And she didn't want to miss out on seeing the Mall while it was free of the usual throngs of tourists.

Eddie laughed and said, "I like your spirit."

They watched the raindrops hit the still surface of the Mall's reflecting pool, breaking up the strange, elongated image of the Washington Monument.

When they reached the Lincoln Memorial, they stood at the base of the steps for a moment, taking it all in.

"It's haunting," Nancy said. "That giant statue of a man just sitting there, the light glowing all around him."

Eddie agreed. "He looks like he's thinking things that are so important, the rest of us can't even imagine them."

"Come on," Nancy said, taking Eddie's hand and running up the steps.

Inside the memorial, they were sheltered from the rain. Eddie stood in front of the seated figure of Lincoln, his hand resting on the marble base of the huge chair. "Feel this," he said. "It's so cool and smooth that it's almost soft."

Nancy put her hand on the marble and ran it over the smooth surface. "You're right—" she began. Her words were cut short when a chunk of marble suddenly exploded right where her hand had been. Shards of the sharp rock flew everywhere.

Nancy ducked, covering her eyes.

Instantly, another bit of stone exploded, this time right by Eddie's head. Nancy saw his eyes widen. He rushed toward her now, slamming into her and knocking her to the ground.

When the next bit of marble burst, Nancy heard the distinctive, high-pitched whir of a bullet ricochet accompany it.

"Someone's shooting at us!" she cried.

"We've got to take cover," Eddie said. He had shielded her with his body. Now the two of them scrambled to their knees and scooted to the back of the memorial. They crouched there, using the marble monument as a shield.

"So we *were* being followed," Nancy said.

Eddie nodded. "Are you okay?"

"So far." She peeked around the corner. A man in black clothing, his face covered with a ski mask, emerged from the darkness and stood calmly in a pool of light at the foot of the memorial. He held an automatic pistol with a silencer screwed into the barrel.

Nancy felt Eddie's hand on her back as he peered around also.

"This is not a good situation," Nancy whispered.

"Do you think he is the only one?" Eddie asked.

The shooter stood out in the light, as still as the statue.

"Yes, I think so," Nancy said. "But what is he waiting for? He has us cornered."

As if on cue, the gunman started up the steps. He took them one at a time, carefully scanning the inside of the memorial.

Eddie took his cell phone from the inside pocket of his tux jacket. He flipped it open and dialed. "Omar," he whispered hoarsely. "We're in trouble. Bring the car down to the Lincoln Memorial, pronto."

The gunman was now halfway up the stairs, still acting as cool and casual as a tourist on vacation.

Suddenly, the skies opened and the rain came down harder.

"How long will it take Omar to get here?"

"Thirty seconds, maybe a minute," Eddie said.

Nancy watched the shooter approach. He lifted the handgun up to shoulder level, playing it back and forth, searching.

"We don't have that much time," Nancy whispered. "We have to make a move. The gunman has to come around the statue to find us. As soon as he chooses one side, I say we take off the other way."

Eddie nodded grimly. "Not very good odds, but it's all we've got."

"Wait, maybe not." Nancy turned and scanned the back wall of the memorial. Staying low, she reached out from behind the statue and picked up an empty glass bottle off the floor. "Our one piece of luck," she said, returning to Eddie's side. "The cleaning crew must not show up till morning."

The gunman had reached the top of the stairs. He was less than twenty feet away.

Nancy and Eddie stayed back behind Lincoln; if they tried to look out the man would certainly see them. They had to wait, watching for the man's shadow. Nancy felt her heart racing. She held the bottle poised in her right hand.

Then the long, distorted shadow of a man appeared, stretching out along the right side of Lincoln's chair.

Before the man could round the corner, Eddie and Nancy took off, sprinting around the other side of the statue.

They made it to the steps before Nancy heard the muffled *whump* of the silenced gun. A bullet sang past her ear.

She stopped and pivoted, whipping the bottle back behind her blindly.

She saw the masked gunman duck, and she and Eddie took off again, bounding down the steps two and three at a time. Nancy could only hope the flying bottle was enough of a distraction to stall the man.

Eddie held her by the hand as they dashed for the darkness and safety of Constitution Avenue. Bullets rang off the cement walkway at their feet.

Then, out of the night, they spotted the limousine. Omar slammed the brakes as the car pulled alongside them. The back door opened and they dove in—the car hadn't even come to a stop.

Omar gunned the engine. The tires squealed and smoked, and the door slammed shut just as two more slugs bit into the bulletproof glass.

Nancy and Eddie both gasped for air. Looking out the rear window, Nancy saw the gunman standing by the side of the road, growing smaller as they sped away.

"You two okay?" Omar called back over his shoulder.

"Yes," Eddie said, relief obvious in his voice. "Yes, I think so."

He turned to Nancy. "Now do you believe I had nothing to do with stealing the hummingbird?"

Nancy just looked into his earnest green eyes. "Yes," she said honestly. "I believe you." She had doubted him when she saw the tattoo, but that was over.

"Whoever stole the hummingbird has just added attempted murder to his list of accomplishments," Eddie said. "This has to have something to do with the negotiations."

Nancy's newfound trust prompted her to tell Eddie about the attack in the parking garage, which increased his anger.

"I have to talk to my father about this," he said. "We'll need much more security around when the president of San Valente arrives for the ceremony tomorrow."

"You're right," Nancy said. "We don't know who else could be a target."

"We have several guest bedrooms at the embassy," Eddie said. "Let me take you there so you'll be safe tonight."

"No," Nancy said. "I have to make sure George is okay."

"Both of you can stay there."

"We'll be fine," Nancy assured him.

Eddie continued to try to convince Nancy to stay at the embassy with him and his parents, but she politely declined.

When they dropped her off at George's town house, Eddie walked her to the door while Omar stood lookout at the front of the car.

"I'll wait until I see your light go on upstairs," Eddie said, as Nancy unlocked the door.

"Be careful," Nancy said after she pushed the door open. The ordeal they had shared had brought them closer together, and they exchanged a quick hug and kiss good night.

Nancy watched from the upstairs window as the limo drove off, then went to check on George. Her friend was sleeping soundly, a peaceful smile on her face.

It took Nancy a long time to fall asleep. The events of the evening kept coming back in vivid detail. Finally, though, she fell into a fitful sleep.

Something woke her while it was still dark. She listened intently. Yes, there it was. Someone was ringing the doorbell over and over.

Nancy glanced at her alarm clock. It was four in the morning. She put on a robe and stumbled downstairs as the doorbell echoed through the house. She peered through the peephole in the front door cautiously.

It was Eddie, standing in the pouring rain, his jacket pulled over his head.

Nancy yanked open the door. "What is it, Eddie? What's going on?"

"It's my father," Eddie said, his voice shaking with fear and anger. "He's been kidnapped."

11

Kidnapped!

Nancy grabbed Eddie by the sleeve and pulled him inside. He was soaked to the bone.

"Tell me what happened!" she said urgently.

Eddie sat down on the couch, then jumped up, as if suddenly remembering how wet he was. Nancy motioned for him to sit.

"No. I can think better on my feet anyway." He wiped the rain off his face with the palms of his hands. "The kidnappers just called my mother at the embassy. She's hysterical, and no one can get the story straight. She's just so terrified and confused."

"Who do you think is responsible?" Nancy asked.

"If it's anyone I used to know with the Night Fighters, I'll make sure they don't get away with this." He clenched his fists. "I'll go back to San Valente and track them down myself."

"But when did it happen?" Nancy asked. "Just now?"

"No," Eddie replied. "My parents dropped George off and then went back to the embassy. My father has a habit of going out for the early edition of the newspaper on nights when they come home late from a party or something." Eddie shook his fists in the air. "He likes to walk to the newspaper stand by himself. He knows he shouldn't do it, but he goes anyway."

Nancy could imagine all too clearly what had happened. "Someone grabbed him off the street?"

"That's the only way it could've happened," Eddie said. "My mother got worried when he didn't come back after half an hour or so. Then, at about two o'clock this morning, she got the call."

"What about the police?"

"The guy who called said that if we contact them, he'd kill my father."

"Let me get dressed," Nancy said. "I'll be down in a minute."

Upstairs, she looked in on George. Nancy figured her friend must've been totally exhausted

112

after a day of being sick and an evening of dancing. She left a short note on the dresser, telling George she'd be at the San Valente embassy.

When she went back downstairs, she was dressed in jeans, tennis shoes, and a University of Chicago sweatshirt—a gift from her own father. She hoped it would bring them luck in getting Eddie's dad back safe and sound.

Omar drove them through the wet, nearly deserted streets. Soon they turned down a broad boulevard lined with colonial mansions. The buildings had all been converted to embassies for various countries around the world. Stone and wrought-iron gates surrounded the houses, and national flags flew high above the carefully landscaped lawns.

Omar slowed and turned into a driveway. He nodded to the gate attendant and continued through to a circular drive that curved in front of the San Valente embassy. All the lights inside seemed to be on.

Eddie's mother was upstairs in the library, surrounded by embassy staff. Her eyes were puffy from crying, but she still maintained a determined dignity.

"Eddie, Nancy," she said, coming forward to greet them. "The kidnapper called again while you were gone."

"If he calls back, send the call up here to the library," Eddie said to the staff. "No one talks to this guy but me, understand?"

The staff members nodded in silence. Eddie sternly ordered them out of the room, and they retreated.

Once they were alone in the room, Eddie and Nancy led Mrs. Enriquez over to a sofa and sat down.

"What did the kidnapper say this time?" Eddie asked.

Mrs. Enriquez clutched at a silk handkerchief. Nancy noticed that it was embroidered with her husband's initials.

"He said that your father is an insurance policy to make sure the economic treaty falls apart," Mrs. Enriquez said. She turned to Nancy. "If the president signs the agreement tonight at the state dinner, they're going to shoot my husband."

"*Los Luchadores!*" Eddie exclaimed. "It must be them."

Nancy turned to the ambassador's wife. "What else did the caller say? Did you notice any kind of accent, anything unusual?"

"No. No accent. He spoke through some kind of electronic voice synthesizer." Tears started to run down Mrs. Enriquez's cheeks. "He sounded so frightening, like a machine."

"It's okay, Mom," Eddie said, putting his arm around her shoulder. "We'll find him before anything happens."

The phone on a small writing desk rang. Mrs. Enriquez jumped and held the handkerchief to her mouth.

Eddie let the phone ring one more time before he went over and picked up. At Nancy's prompting, he turned on the speakerphone.

A toneless, computer-altered voice filled the room. "Eduardo Enriquez?" it said.

"Speaking."

Nancy could see Eddie's knuckles whiten as his grip tightened on the arms of his chair.

"We have spoken to your mother. Now we are giving you the message, so things will be perfectly clear. Understand?"

Nancy walked over to the writing table so she could see Eddie's face. "What do you want from me?" he asked.

"If everything goes as planned, your father will be released unharmed after the state dinner tonight. But it is your job to make sure things go as planned."

The computer voice continued: "The president of San Valente arrives late this afternoon. Therefore, he will not discover that his gift to the United

115

States, *El Pajaro*, has been lost until only an hour before the signing ceremony.

"We are counting on this to cause enough confusion and embarrassment to call off the ceremony," the voice continued. "If you tell anyone about us, your father dies. The signing must officially be called off because of the theft, not the kidnapping of the San Valente ambassador."

Eddie raised one eyebrow and glanced over at Nancy. "What if it doesn't work?" he said into the phone. "What if the president signs anyway?"

A silence of a few seconds followed.

The voice came back on the line. "Then your father dies."

Eddie opened his mouth to speak, but was interrupted.

"We will call back soon with the details of your father's release." There was a loud click, then only the dial tone.

Eddie dropped his arm listlessly to his side, still holding on to the phone receiver. Nancy went to him and gently lifted the phone from his hand, placing it back in its cradle.

Over the next few hours, while they waited for the kidnapper to call again, Eddie paced the room, thinking out loud.

"I know the president of San Valente," he said. "He's a very emotional man. You know, lots of pride, especially for our little country. But I don't know what he will do. He might go ahead with the agreement."

Nancy sat on the sofa with Mrs. Enriquez, comforting her. "Can you get to the president? Can you tell him your father's in danger?"

"No," Eddie said. "The kidnapper specifically warned against that."

"He said the *official* reason had to be the theft," Nancy said. "What if we tell the president about your father but get him to report to the press that the reason he's not going to sign is the missing gift?"

"I don't know," Eddie said, holding his head in his hands. He turned and retraced his steps across the carpet in frustration. "I don't know what to do. I'm afraid they'll kill my father no matter what happens."

At eight o'clock in the morning they were no closer to a resolution about what to do. The rain had stopped, and bright sunshine came in through the windows. Embassy staffers brought in coffee and pastries, but Eddie and his mother were too upset to drink or eat anything.

Nancy excused herself and went out in the hall to call George. She dialed the town house first but got no answer. Next, she dialed George's office line. On the second ring, she picked up.

"George, it's Nancy."

"Nan! Are you still at the embassy? What's up?"

"Nothing I can talk about over the phone," Nancy said. "I just wanted to see if you were okay."

"I'm fine," George answered. "But Brent's sitting here with me in my office, and he's scared to death."

Nancy felt her breath catch in her throat. "Go on."

"He was working late last night," George said. "Someone called him. The caller said he knew Brent had been telling people about the bird being stolen."

"But he only told Eddie, right?"

"Right. But somehow somebody found out. The caller said if he tells anyone else before the state dinner tonight, his life is in danger."

Nancy took a stab in the dark. "Did Brent recognize the voice?"

"That was the really scary part, according to Brent. The person sounded like a talking computer—totally eerie and inhuman."

"Tell Brent to stay cool," Nancy said.

"Yeah. The problem is that Bureau Chief Bingham keeps calling him," George said. "She's demanding to see the bird before the ceremony, and she's starting to get really suspicious about his excuses. So I told him to stay here in my office where no one can find him."

"Good thinking. I'll call you back soon, okay?"

Nancy hung up. She was relieved that she could eliminate Brent as a suspect. There was obviously no way he could call in kidnapping threats if he was holed up in George's office.

When she returned to the library, Eddie was back on the phone.

"I want to speak to my father," he said. "How do I know he's okay if you won't let me speak to him."

"It isn't necessary," the voice replied.

Eddie's words crackled with anger. "If you don't put my father on the line right now, I'm going to go to the White House and tell them that the bird was stolen. I'm going to tell them that it was stolen by an insider working with the Night Fighters of San Valente. The press will say that it's my country's fault, not the fault of the United States." Eddie was shouting into the phone now. "How does that fit with your perfect plan?"

The line went silent. At first, Nancy was afraid that the kidnapper had hung up. But then they heard sounds in the background. The computer voice said something, then a man replied.

A voice came over the line. It started speaking Spanish for a second or two, then was cut off.

"Dad!" Eddie said.

They heard the synthesized voice in the background say, "Speak English, nothing else."

Eddie's father came back on the line, his voice weary and thin with strain. "My son."

"Dad?"

"Son, listen to me and remember what I say. Soon you will be twenty-four years old, well past the gateway to manhood—"

"Hurry it up. Just tell them you're okay," the kidnapper said from the background.

Eddie's father continued. "It isn't anyone's fault. What happens to me is water under the bridge. Just take care of your three sisters for me now."

The inhuman voice came back. "Satisfied? If things go smoothly, we will drop your father off within walking distance of the embassy sometime after ten o'clock tonight."

"Don't you hurt him," Eddie said, his teeth set in rage.

"Don't do anything stupid," the voice warned. "If one little thing goes wrong, your father pays the price."

The line went dead.

12

A Code and a Clue

Nancy expected Eddie to slam the phone back down, but he replaced it carefully. He rubbed at his unshaven chin, lost in concentration. Mrs. Enriquez's quiet sobs were the only sound in the room.

"Eddie, what are you thinking?" Nancy asked.

Eddie sat in a chair at the writing desk and started frantically jotting down notes. "Come here," he said to Nancy.

She stood right next to him, reading over his shoulder. He'd written down the numbers twenty-four and three, as well as several words and incomplete phrases.

Nancy immediately realized what he was doing.

121

"You're trying to remember exactly what your father said, aren't you?"

"Yes," Eddie replied. "That was one of the first things he said—'remember what I say.' Can you help me remember the rest, Nancy?"

Nancy dragged a side chair over and sat down next to Eddie. "The first thing he did was call you son," she said.

"Right. And he almost never does that. Everything he said was sort of weird. It didn't make any sense."

"He said you were almost twenty-four," Mrs. Enriquez added, coming up and putting her hands on her son's shoulders. "But he knows very well you're only twenty-one."

"Yeah." Eddie looked up at his mother. "And he told me to take care of my three sisters." He shifted his gaze to Nancy. "I have two younger brothers."

"He sent you some kind of coded message," Nancy said. She could barely contain her excitement. "What else did he say, exactly?"

Eddie read what he'd written down. "'You are at the gateway to manhood.'"

"He said, 'You're well past the gateway to manhood,'" Eddie's mother corrected.

Eddie wrote that down.

"He said it wasn't anyone's fault what happened to him," Nancy said. "He said it was water under the bridge."

Eddie kept scribbling. "Then he ended with the thing about the three sisters."

"Get it organized," Nancy said. "Get it all back in the right order."

Eddie crossed something out, then read the piecemeal transcription aloud.

"Son, remember what I say. Soon you will be twenty-four years old, well past the gateway to manhood. What happens to me isn't anyone's fault. It's just water under the bridge. Take care of your three sisters for me."

"What does it mean?" Eddie's mother asked.

Eddie placed the paper on the desk where they could all see it.

Nancy read it over three or four times. The wording wasn't exactly what the ambassador had said, but it would have to do. "He hid the message within these words," she said. "What we have to do is separate the coded information from all the junk around it."

Eddie reached over with his pen and circled the twenty-four and the three. "We know that the numbers are important because he made such a big point of getting them wrong."

After a few more readings, Nancy saw a pattern

begin to emerge. "There's one bit of valuable information in each phrase or statement," she said. "The first line told Eddie to memorize what his father was about to say. The second line gave us the number twenty-four."

Eddie's mother let out a small cry of anguish. "The fourth line," she said. "The one about it being nobody's fault. I think he's trying to tell us that the kidnappers are going to kill him no matter what. Whatever we do, he dies."

Nancy wished she could tell Mrs. Enriquez she was wrong, but she feared that her interpretation was correct.

"We know the sixth line contains the number three," Nancy said. "That leaves the third and fifth lines."

Eddie crossed everything else out and read just those lines: " 'Well past the gateway to manhood. It's just water under the bridge.' "

The words "gateway" and "water" caught Nancy's attention. She stood up so fast her chair fell over behind her. "The Watergate complex," she said, naming the infamous Washington landmark. "That's where they're holding him."

Eddie jumped up and hugged her. "Room two-forty-three—that has to be it."

Mrs. Enriquez rushed over and kissed Nancy's

cheek. "There's still a chance!" she exclaimed. "Still a chance to get him back alive."

Eddie's mother wanted to call the police and give them the information, but Eddie adamantly refused. "We need to make sure this information is correct," he said. "What if the room number is really three-twenty-four? We don't want the police running all over the place, knocking on doors and tipping off the kidnappers. Nancy and I will check things out quietly." He hugged his mother as they prepared to leave the library. "We'll call in help as soon as we know where Dad is."

Omar met them outside with the car. It was midmorning, and rush hour traffic had thinned. Omar made good time as he headed toward the river, weaving the limo expertly past cars and around pedestrians and bicycle messengers.

The enormous Watergate complex was right on the Potomac, about halfway between Georgetown and the Roosevelt Bridge. They came up on it from New Hampshire Avenue, and Nancy recognized it immediately from photos she'd seen. The building followed the bend of the river, its stacked layers of slab concrete and smoked glass curving to conform to the bank.

They didn't want to risk the limo being recognized by someone in the parking lot, so Omar parked on the street. The three of them entered under the canopy of the main entrance. It was just about checkout time. Consequently, the lobby was packed with busloads of children on school trips and elderly tourists. A bank of six elevators lined the wall to the right.

Using a line of chattering kids as cover, Omar, Nancy, and Eddie slipped into an empty elevator just as the doors sighed closed. Eddie pushed the button for the second floor.

For the first time, Nancy noticed that Omar wasn't wearing his chauffeur's uniform. He still had on a sport coat, though, and as the elevator headed up, she found out why.

He pulled the lapel of his blazer back and pulled out a snub-nosed revolver. After checking the cylinder to make certain the gun was loaded, he put it back in its holster.

Nancy shot Eddie a look. This meant they were going to do a lot more than just make sure they had the right information. Eddie and Omar were ready for a battle.

"You okay?" Eddie whispered.

"Ready for anything," Nancy replied.

The doors opened and they held back for a second, while Omar checked the hallway. He then gestured for them to exit the elevator.

A sign of room numbers directed them to the

left. Twenty-five yards down the hall, they found room number 243. As soon as they got to it, they heard voices coming from inside. Nancy put her ear to the door.

". . . we've only got a one-hour window," someone was saying. The voice sounded familiar to Nancy, but she couldn't quite place it.

The person inside seemed to be talking on the phone. "No," the voice said. "You get here by then or the deal's off. If you aren't here, the ambassador is in serious trouble."

She stepped back from the door, nodding silently to Omar and Eddie to tell them they had the right place.

Eddie rapped his knuckles hard on the door.

"Who's there?" the man inside called out.

"Housekeeping," Eddie said. "Clean towels for you here."

"Just leave them out in the hall."

"Very good, sir."

Now Eddie motioned for Nancy and Omar to clear away from the door. Nancy flattened herself against the wall—she didn't want the kidnapper spotting her through the wide-angle peephole.

Less than a minute later, they heard the safety chain being unhooked.

Nancy didn't dare breathe.

The door opened barely an inch, then stopped.

Nancy wondered what the guy would do when he didn't see any towels on the floor.

But the one-inch opening was all Omar needed. He stepped out from the wall and executed a powerful front kick. Nancy heard the steel-framed door slam into the man inside. Instantly, she came out of her hiding place and rushed into the room.

The kidnapper was just getting to his feet. He was dressed in black slacks and a black turtleneck. Nancy recognized him as the man who'd tried to gun them down the night before. He had the ski cap rolled up on his head. But before Nancy could get a look at his face, he yanked the cap back down.

Nancy spotted the kidnapper's gun on the TV stand against the back wall. She dove for his feet, trying to trip him before he could reach the weapon.

He was too quick. When she saw that he'd grabbed the automatic, Nancy rolled behind the bed. The gun went off twice, but they were wild shots. She stayed low.

Then she saw Omar's feet flash past as he dashed into the room. There was a blur of sound: grunts, kicks, a chair turning over, then another high-pitched whine from the gun's silencer.

Nancy risked a peek over the edge of the bed. Omar was down, and he lay very still.

Eddie struggled in the far corner with the kidnapper, both his hands locked on the gunman's wrist.

Knowing she had mere seconds, Nancy rushed to the nightstand beside the bed. She grabbed the antique brass lamp from the nightstand with one hand and yanked the cord from the wall with the other.

Eddie saw her coming and worked the gunman around so his back was to her. She lifted the heavy lamp high and brought it crashing down on the kidnapper's head.

She only stunned him.

He staggered back just enough for Eddie to escape from the corner. A split second later the man was alert again. He spun to face Nancy.

She cracked a crisp side kick into his wrist, sending the pistol flying.

Then she made a near fatal mistake—she reached for the ski mask.

The kidnapper swung wildly, clubbing her in the side of the head with his arm. She fell to her knees.

She closed her eyes and tried to protect herself from the crushing blow she expected any second. She kept waiting. Nothing. She opened her eyes.

The kidnapper had vanished.

13

The Truth Is Revealed

"He got away!" Eddie yelled to Nancy. "Let's go. Omar—"

In all the confusion, Eddie hadn't realized that Omar had been hurt. He rushed to his friend and shouted, "Omar!" Frantically, he pulled the cell phone from his pocket and dialed 911.

While Eddie talked to the dispatcher, Nancy knelt down beside the limo driver. His breathing and pulse were strong. He'd been hit in the thick part of his shoulder, and though there was a lot of blood, it looked as if he'd be okay with proper medical attention.

Nancy looked up at Eddie. "You stay with Omar. I'm going after that guy."

"No. It's too dangerous." Eddie tried to grab her arm as she ran past, but she wrenched free.

Nancy paused outside the hallway. She had to think like a kidnapper. What would he do?

He was wearing a ski mask on a summer day. That was too conspicuous—he'd never risk riding the elevator.

Nancy ran for the stairs.

She flew down the stairwell, noting each floor as she descended. The kidnapper would park his car someplace dark and quiet. Doubling her speed, she continued down to the second level of the underground garage.

Nancy burst through the fire door just in time to see a black sedan flash past, engine roaring. Nancy chased the car for a few steps, then gave up. The sedan rounded the corner, and she knew the kidnapper had gotten away.

But not before she'd memorized the license plate.

She rode the elevator back up to the second floor and ran back to the room.

Conscious now, Omar sat up against the side of the bed, a pillowcase wrapped tightly around his shoulder.

"Eddie?" Nancy called.

Omar nodded toward the bathroom. "In there, with his father."

Loose ropes and used duct tape lay in a tangle on the bathroom floor. Eddie and his father were embraced in a hug, the ambassador clapping his son heartily on the back.

"There she is!" the ambassador exclaimed, releasing his son. "Thank goodness you're safe, Nancy!" Mr. Enriquez had a dark bruise above his right eye, but other than that he appeared healthy and unhurt.

"I'm just glad we got here in time," Nancy said.

"You aren't the only one," the ambassador replied. "If you hadn't figured out my message, well, I don't even want to think about what would have happened."

They heard a knock on the outside door. Two paramedics came into the hotel room carrying their equipment. They went right to work on Omar's wound.

One of the paramedics glanced up as he hung an IV drip. "This looks like a gunshot wound," he said. "Which means I've got to call the police."

"Yeah, get them in here," Eddie said. "We've got quite a story to tell." He sat down next to Omar. "Take good care of this guy," he said to the paramedics. "I want him around for a while."

Nancy asked the ambassador if he would come out to the hall for a moment. When they stepped outside, they surprised a woman trying to get a peek in the room. The woman hurried away.

Nancy faced the ambassador. They talked quietly, huddled together. "How many were there? Do you know?"

"Two, I think," Eddie's father said. "They grabbed me right off the street last night. Gave me this lump on my head," he added, pointing to the swollen mark.

"Did you get a good look at them?"

"No. They were both wearing ski masks. One was bigger, more muscular—the one you tangled with just now."

Nancy asked if they'd given away any useful information about their plans. "Did they accidentally use each other's names or anything?"

"No names," Mr. Enriquez said. "I would have remembered that. But the big fellow was very worried about something. He said over and over again that they only had one hour to get the hummingbird. 'A one-hour window,' he kept saying."

"A one-hour window . . ." Nancy repeated, more to herself than anyone else. "Where have I heard something like that before?"

Then it came to her. The security memo she'd seen on Agent Marks's computer. The White

House security system is scheduled to be down today between one and two in the afternoon! she realized, her heartbeat quickening.

She checked her watch. The time was 12:15.

"Eddie," Nancy said, leaning into the room. "We've got to get to the White House, now."

"What is it?" Eddie asked, coming out into the hall.

"The hummingbird is still in the White House," Nancy said. "Whoever stole it couldn't get it out because of the metal detectors. But the security system is going to be shut off in forty-five minutes for maintenance. That's when the thieves will try to sneak it out somehow."

Nancy heard sirens outside. "The police are here," she said. "We don't have time to answer questions."

"Don't worry," Mr. Enriquez said. "I'll talk to them, and then I'll ride to the hospital with Omar."

Eddie and Nancy used the stairs to get down to the lobby and sneaked out of the hotel as two officers stepped into an elevator.

After finding the limousine, Eddie got behind the wheel and Nancy jumped into the passenger seat. Eddie whipped the big car around and headed back up New Hampshire Avenue.

"What'd you figure out?" he asked.

"At least one of the kidnappers is a Secret Service agent," Nancy said. "Maybe even Agent Marks, chief of Residence Security."

Drivers in front of them seemed to respectfully move out of the way as Eddie tore down the road. He swung onto Pennsylvania Avenue and stepped on the gas pedal.

"I saw a memo in Marks's office yesterday, talking about how the security system was going to be down for maintenance today," Nancy continued. "It was supposed to be top secret, sent only to other agents. And then your dad overheard one of the kidnappers mention a 'one-hour window' to get *El Pajaro* out."

Eddie cranked the steering wheel hard to the left, then stomped on the brakes. The limousine came screeching to a stop just inches short of the White House south entrance gate.

The same young marine who'd questioned Nancy's pass the morning before sprang out of the guard house, rifle in hand. "What's going on?" he yelled. "Get out of the car. Hands where I can see them."

Nancy got out with her hands in the air. "It's me," she said. "You remember me from yesterday?"

The marine didn't move. "Yes, it's Ms. Drew, right?"

"And this is Eddie Enriquez," Nancy said as he emerged from the car.

"I know him too," the soldier replied. "His father's the ambassador from San Valente. What's the problem?"

Nancy put her hands down. "We need your help," she said.

Less than a minute later, the three of them were standing in the guardhouse watching a computer screen. The marine typed in the license number of the government plate Nancy had memorized.

"That car's registered to the Secret Service," the soldier said. "Right now it's being used by an agent named Don Marks."

Nancy felt Eddie squeeze her hand. They knew for sure who one of the kidnappers was. They just had to find Marks and his accomplice before the two men slipped out of the White House with the hummingbird and disappeared forever.

"We have a problem," Nancy said. "We need access to the main house, maybe even the residence. Marks's accomplice might also be a Secret Service agent. Who can we trust to get us in?"

"You're forgetting something," Eddie said. "My mother and father have stayed in the White House as the president's guests. I can get up there, no problem."

The young marine looked concerned. "Is there

136

something going on?" he asked. "Something I should know about?" He started to pick up his phone.

Nancy's watch read 12:35. She didn't have the time to explain everything. "Can you leave your post?"

"Absolutely not," the young man said. "Not under any condition."

Nancy had to take a chance. "Are you friends with any Secret Service agents?"

"Sure. I've gotten to know a few of them pretty well."

"Call the one you trust the most," Nancy said. "Tell him to meet us at the entrance to the West Wing. And ask him not to tell anyone else."

The marine's blue eyes narrowed as he gave Nancy a hard stare. "I'm not going to get in trouble for this?"

"I promise you won't."

As the soldier picked up the phone to make the call, Nancy and Eddie sprinted across the South Lawn to the West Wing.

A young agent with the trim build of a long-distance runner met them there, holding the door open for them.

"I'm Agent Walsh," he said. "Mike at the guardhouse told me something's up."

"Take us to Agent Marks's office," Nancy said. "I'll explain as much of it as I can on the way."

The first thing she asked Agent Walsh was if he'd heard about the gift from San Valente being stolen.

"Not a word," Walsh replied.

That was just as Nancy had suspected. Marks had only pretended to alert other agents. He'd hidden the statue somewhere and kept quiet about it.

Nancy could relay only a few more details before they were standing outside Marks's office. She didn't expect him to be in, and he wasn't.

"Hold it!" his secretary said. "You were here yesterday. Agent Marks never had an appointment with you."

Nancy ignored the woman as she tried unsuccessfully to keep them from entering the inner office.

"What are you looking for?" Eddie asked.

"Anything," Nancy replied, flipping through a stack of papers on Marks's desk. "Something to link him to his accomplice. Something to tell us where he hid the . . ." Her voice trailed off as she spotted the white plaster church on the credenza.

Marks had managed to glue the whole thing back together. Nancy picked up the scene and

examined it closely. It was perfectly pieced together—the men shaking hands across the pew,
the children laughing, the women dressed in fancy
coats and hats.

She set the delicate casting down carefully. "I
know where the hummingbird is," she said.

14

A Frantic Finish

Eddie was by her side. "Where? Where'd they hide the hummingbird?"

"In the Lincoln bedroom," Nancy replied, glancing at her watch. "And it's almost one o'clock."

With Agent Walsh, Eddie and Nancy sprinted up the first floor of the West Wing, then through the long colonnade to the residence. As they approached the Secret Service agent stationed at the west entrance hall, he stood up. He stepped out toward them, then recognized Walsh.

"Everything okay, John?"

Walsh stopped. Nancy wondered what was going on. Had they gotten unlucky and picked the wrong agent to trust?

"We may have a problem," Walsh said to the other agent. "Send a couple of men—the best guys—up to the nest right now. Tell them to seal off the Lincoln Suite but stay out of sight. Keep the eggs warm."

The three continued down the hall. Nancy glanced back over her shoulder and saw the agent speaking into a walkie-talkie.

"Eggs?" she said.

Walsh turned to her and, without smiling, said, "The president and first lady. That's what we call them."

They took a wide set of stairs at the back of the mansion. At the first-floor landing, Nancy caught a glimpse of the vast East Room, empty except for an enormous grand piano set back in the corner.

Then they were on the second floor—the private residence of the First Family.

They paused in the carpeted hallway that ran the entire length of the second floor. This part of the White House looked less like a museum and more like the home of someone rich and powerful. Family portraits hung on the walls. Nancy spotted one of Muffin's chew toys—a pink rubber bone— lying in the middle of the hall. Nancy didn't hear any activity. There was complete silence.

Eddie had been in the residence before. He and Walsh moved quietly down the hall to the left, with Nancy following. Eddie whispered to Nancy, "This end of the house has the guest rooms."

The Lincoln Suite covered the southeastern corner of the house. It consisted of two rooms, a large bedroom with a smaller sitting room through a doorway to the left.

"I don't see anything," Walsh said in a low voice. "So now what?"

But Nancy had already spotted what she was looking for. The bedroom had two long windows in the south-facing wall. Between them stood a marble-topped rosewood table. The replacement plaster church scene Nancy had seen Brent carrying around two days ago sat on the table, the detailed figures illuminated by the early afternoon sunlight. That meant the kidnappers hadn't yet come to get the stolen hummingbird.

"Now we wait," Nancy said. "Whoever stole the hummingbird only has an hour to get it past security." She went through the narrow door leading to the sitting room, motioning for Eddie and Walsh to follow.

"I hope you know what you're doing," Walsh said. "Maybe we should just find Agent Marks and see what his side of the story is."

Eddie gripped Walsh's arm. "She knows what she's doing, believe me."

They hid on either side of the sitting room doorway. From her vantage point, Nancy had a full view of the Lincoln bedroom. A queen-sized bed with an extremely tall, carved headboard was next to the entrance, opposite the windows. Matching rosewood chairs and a dresser completed the set.

Nancy wished she was as confident as Eddie. She hoped her hunch was right—everything seemed to fit—but she could have missed something along the way. The kidnappers could be escaping at that very moment. They might be sitting smugly on an airplane thirty thousand feet over the ocean, the solid gold bird tucked safely inside the luggage compartment.

Then she heard a noise: a whisper, or a shoe lightly scuffing along the carpet.

Out of the corner of her eye, Nancy saw Agent Walsh tense up. His jacket lapel was pulled back, revealing the butt of a gun.

Nancy ducked her head back just as Agent Marks entered the bedroom. She felt Eddie move beside her and grabbed his wrist. "Wait," she whispered.

They watched as Agent Marks, dressed in his normal Secret Service suit and tie, strode across the bedroom to the rosewood table. He picked up the plaster scene, carefully cradling it in one strong arm.

Then another person entered the room.

Nancy stared in disbelief. Security Council officer Todd Willis stood by the foot of the bed, motioning for Marks to hurry up.

Nancy nodded, and Agent Walsh stepped through the door of the sitting room, his gun leveled at Marks's chest.

"It's over, Don," he said firmly. "Put that thing down on the floor and hand me your gun."

Marks seemed startled but quickly recovered. He edged closer to Todd. "Agent Walsh," he said, smiling. "I think there's been a slight misunderstanding."

Nancy and Eddie stepped out next to Walsh.

"No, I don't think so," Nancy said. "You stole the statue of the hummingbird from the Diplomatic Reception Room two days ago." She turned to Willis. "Or was it you who hit me over the head, Todd?"

Willis had gone pale. He stood still, in complete shock.

"That's crazy," Marks said. He took a few steps closer to Willis and handed him the plaster tableau. "I've worked here for fifteen years, Ms.

Drew. Agent Walsh knows I'd never do anything like that."

Agent Walsh had his gun on Marks. A look of doubt flashed in his eyes. He glanced over at Nancy. The five of them were facing off now, Marks and Willis not more than six feet from Nancy, Eddie, and Walsh.

"So what *are* you doing here?" Walsh asked.

"Brent Larson sent us up," Marks said. "Apparently the woman who donated this piece of artwork had a change of heart. She wants it back."

Nancy felt that Walsh had a spark of doubt.

"Put your gun away, Walsh," Agent Marks said.

She saw Walsh hesitate, lowering his arms a few inches, taking his aim off Marks. His eyes locked with Nancy's, and she saw the doubt in them.

Nancy knew she had to act, and fast. Marks and Willis were headed for the door.

Without hesitation, she kicked hard, aiming for the plaster scene that Todd held in his arms. The piece fell to the floor, shattering. Willis fell backward onto the floor, stunned.

Nancy was poised, ready to nail Marks or Willis again.

But something flew past her. It was Eddie. He dove forward, putting his shoulder into Marks's chest and driving him to the floor.

Then Walsh was standing over Marks, pinning him to the floor with his foot.

It was over.

Nancy took a deep breath. "No," she said, looking down at Marks. "There was no misunderstanding at all." She pointed to the middle of the floor, where the golden hummingbird lay amid a sea of shattered plaster.

Within seconds, four other agents swarmed into the room. One of them picked up Willis, who was staggering and shaking his head, as if he didn't understand what had just happened.

When he gathers his wits, Nancy thought, he's going to have a lot of explaining to do.

Later that night the state dinner went off without a hitch. A black limousine, compliments of the White House, picked up Nancy, George, and Brent and whisked them through the southwest gate. The girls merely flashed their passes, and the uniformed officers smiled and waved them on through.

The limo came to a stop at the top of the drive, and the door was opened for them by a man in a black tuxedo.

"The White House looks so beautiful all lit up at night," Nancy said, as she stepped out of the car. She wore an elegant gold metallic dress, her long hair reflecting the sparkle of the gown.

George followed in a black-sequined ankle-length gown that accentuated her long, graceful figure.

Brent grinned. "Nothing could be as beautiful as the two of you," he said, escorting the girls under the canopied entrance and into the White House.

They followed a stream of finely dressed guests through a reception room on the ground floor, under the vaulted ceiling in the hall, and up the steps to the State Dining Room.

Through the crush of people, Nancy caught Eddie's eye. He'd told her earlier that he'd be required to sit with his parents during dinner, but he was now fighting through the crowd to get to her.

He took Nancy's hands and kissed her on the cheek. "Isn't this amazing?" he asked.

Nancy could only nod in agreement.

"Did you hear?" Eddie asked, looking at his three friends. "Don Marks isn't saying anything to the police, but Todd Willis spilled his guts. He gave up everything."

"Why'd they do it?" Brent asked.

"Marks did it for the oldest reason in the world," Eddie replied.

"What? Love?" George asked crinkling up her nose.

Eddie laughed. "No, George. Money."

"Yeah," Brent added. "That bird would fetch millions on the black market. That was a slick plan they had."

"I still don't get it," George said. "The bird was inside the *Neighboring Pews* scene?"

"Yeah," Brent replied. "I got a chance to look at it this afternoon. Willis told me that a maid broke the first one, but that must've been part of the plan all along. Marks had cut a hole in the bottom of the replacement I found."

"So Marks actually cracked Nancy over the head, took the statue upstairs, and hid it in the replacement? I can't believe the head of security would do such a thing."

"Sad, but true," Brent said. "And the plan was to sneak the bird out of the White House like that. Then they'd take the old one that Marks repaired and put it back in the Lincoln Bedroom. No one would've ever known the difference."

"But what was Todd's angle?"

"Professional jealousy," Eddie said. "He wanted Bureau Chief Bingham's job. He figured that after the treaty fell through at the last minute, Chief Bingham would get fired, and he'd have the best shot at getting appointed to her position."

"He always acted like he was doing all the important work anyway," George noted. "I guess he was desperate for recognition and respect."

"Well, he got the recognition at least," Nancy said. "Stealing a priceless artifact, attempted murder, kidnapping an ambassador—he and Marks make Darcy O'Neill's back-stabbing antics look like a joke. About the only crime they didn't commit was mugging George's boss. That was actually a mugger whom the police have been searching for all year. He's finally been apprehended."

A tall woman emerged from the crowd. Nancy instantly recognized Chief Bingham.

"Ms. Drew, I believe I owe you an apology," she said. "I was rude to you in Todd's office yesterday, and now I come to find out you've done us all a great service." She looked at them each in turn. "You've all helped save this administration from a terrible embarrassment."

Bingham reached into her purse and pulled out a black lacquer fountain pen tipped with gold. "This is a gift from the president. It's a pen he used to sign the treaty earlier this evening," she said. She handed the pen to Nancy. "I want you to have it."

Nancy accepted the pen graciously.

"The president will want to thank you personally," Chief Bingham said. "So don't leave too early."

"Don't worry," Eddie said. "If the president doesn't see us at dinner, we'll be over in the East Room, dancing the night away."

Nancy gave Eddie a jab with her elbow, but Chief Bingham just smiled.

"I'm sure you will," she said. "I'll tell the president to look for the handsomest couple on the floor."

NANCY DREW® MYSTERY STORIES By Carolyn Keene

THE HARDY BOYS® SERIES By Franklin W. Dixon

**Do your younger brothers and sisters
want to read books like yours?**

**Let them know there
are books just for *them!***

They can join Nancy Drew and her best
friends as they collect clues and solve
mysteries in

THE
NANCY DREW
NOTEBOOKS®

Starting with
#1 The Slumber Party Secret
#2 The Lost Locket

AND

**Meet up with suspense and mystery
in Frank and Joe Hardy:
The Clues Brothers™**

#1 The Gross Ghost Mystery
#2 The Karate Clue

FRANK AND JOE HARDY:
THE CLUES
BROTHERS™

Look for a brand-new story every
other month at your local bookseller

A MINSTREL® BOOK

Published by Pocket Books   1366-01

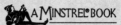